A Reluctance of Blood:
Book 1 of the In-Between

Rebecca M. Senese

Other Books by Rebecca M. Senese

The In-Between Series
Book 2: A Remembrance of Flesh
Book 3: A Retribution of Soul

The Night Killers

Wreck the Halls: 5 Christmas Horror Stories

Oh the Horror! 5 Horror Stories

Bad Ends: 5 Horror Stories

With a Bite: 5 Vampire Tales

The Color of Blood: The Chronicles of Richard Damon

Who Killed Santa? A Christmas / Mystery Novella

A Very Zombie Christmas

The Beginners Guide to the Recently Deceased

Daily Bread

*Forthcoming

A Reluctance of Blood:

Book 1 of the In-Between

Rebecca M. Senese

Published 2013 by RFAR Publishing
Toronto, Canada
http://www.RFARPublishing.com

Trade paper edition designed by Rebecca M. Senese
in InDesign CS5.5

Electronic editions designed by Rebecca M. Senese

Cover design: Rebecca M. Senese
Image © korionov / CanStockPhoto.com
Interior Image © 100ker / DepositPhotos.com

ISBN: 978-1-927603-12-3

A Reluctance of Blood:
Book 1 of the In-Between

Part One: Reluctance

CHAPTER ONE

The April morning dawned clear and cool over the University of Ridgewater campus. Sebastian Lockhart stumbled on the uneven ground as he hurried across the dew-dampened lawn toward class. Around him, the campus was just waking up. Students in light spring jackets, knapsacks or bags slung over their shoulders, bustled along the walkways and across the lawns. The sunshine brightened the brickwork on the older buildings and gleamed on the metal of the newer dorms. The chill air smelled sweet with the mix of new grass and the occasional whiff of smoke from a cigarette.

Sebastian had barely managed a few swallows of coffee on the way out the door. The taste still lingered in his mouth. He wished he'd brought a bottle of water with him but Professor Wilson frowned on any food stuffs in his class. He expected complete attention.

Like that was going to happen at eight thirty in the morning.

Sebastian's own dorm, Saggon Dorm, was one of those newer concrete boxes, plunked down in the center of the campus like a monstrous square among the older Victorian-style buildings. Of course, newer was a relative term. Saggon was forty years old with thick concrete walls, an industrial paint job, and a rickety elevator. But it was right in the middle of the campus, which made getting to class a lot easier.

You'd think after three years, he'd be used to the occasional early morning class by now.

You'd be wrong.

Sebastian's worn running shoes kicked at a knot of dirt as he hurried over the grass. He didn't want to run because his feet would snag on the concrete as soon as he stepped off the dew-slicked grass and he'd end up landing on his head. The few seconds lost on the grass was worth not bashing his head in before the Lansborough Building.

At six three and barely two hundred pounds, Sebastian was all gangly limbs and black hair that stuck out on his head. Uncoordinated felt like it should be his middle name.

At first a purely business college, the Ridgewater campus had originally been laid out in a circle, with the main business buildings in the center. As the school grew, including arts and sciences in its programs, the campus expanded outward, sending out offshoots like the spokes on a wheel. The dorms filled in some of the spaces in between, along with the occasional bar and store. Other spaces were left as green areas with lawns and trees, making it a cozy, comfortable place, if somewhat slippery on mornings when the dew was thick and Sebastian was more uncoordinated than usual.

He reached the asphalt road and sprinted across, heading past Lansborough toward the business building just down the block. The dark red-bricked building loomed on the corner, all four stories. Just another few minutes….

Despite being a required prerequisite for the business program, the only reason Sebastian made it to the eight-thirty morning economics class was the lovely presence of Alexa Hammond. Yet even with the promise of seeing her, he invariably found himself racing to make it on time.

His roommate Charlie never had a class before ten, so Sebastian couldn't rely on Charlie's banging around the dorm room to wake him up. Even with two alarm clocks, one set to a high pitched buzzing that sent the students in the neighboring rooms howling and the other set to a blaring rock station, he somehow always managed to hit the snooze button for each until almost eight o'clock. Then he would jolt upright, heart pounding, sweat shining on his forehead, dampening his black hair that defied gravity and all styling products.

With barely time to jump in and out of the shower at the end of the hall, Sebastian would race back to his room and dive at the small oak dresser his mother had given him, for his first home away from home, she'd said. Underwear, socks, jeans, shirt. He managed to yank the clothing on in seconds, sometimes noticing if there was a mustard stain, sometimes missing it altogether until he was almost at class, almost ready to see Alexa Hammond when the offending stain would leap to his conscious awareness, as if mocking him. A girl like that would *never* go out with a guy with mustard stains on his shirt, it seemed to say to him. What could he possibly be thinking? Then he'd slink into class, hugging his books to his chest, desperate to be on time and ignored, but inevitably a few minutes late and on the receiving end of Professor Wilson's withering glare as he hurried to a seat, still aiming for the row Alexa sat in, if possible.

This particular Thursday, he actually managed to race into class at eight twenty-seven, earning a startled look from Professor Wilson, instead of the usual glare. Sebastian gave a nod to the old man standing at the lectern on the left side of the hall. The lecture seats curved in a semi-circle around the stage, rising upward in staggered steps, allowing every seat an excellent view of the speaker.

As if they wanted an excellent view of the balding top of Professor Wilson's head.

Sebastian walked up the center aisle of the lecture hall, trying to look casual as his gaze searched out Alexa. There she was, tenth row from the top, maybe twenty seats in, looking stylish against the worn blue plaid fabric of the seats. Other students already sat in between the aisle and the row, preventing him from casually wandering into the row for a seat. The next closest was two rows back. He'd never even get a chance to say hello then.

"Hey Sebastian!" Alexa waved at him. She pointed at the seats beside her.

He gave her a slight smile and nod even as his heart started pounding. Just be cool, he thought. He squeezed past the other students to join Alexa.

"Did you read chapters seven through nine?" she said as he sat down in the seat beside her.

Sebastian had to turn his long legs sideways to fit properly in the row. Just not enough leg room here for someone tall, although Sebastian tried not to be too tall. Everyone stared when you were tall, especially since he'd been tall since he was eleven, a real freak of nature.

"I only got through to the beginning of eight," he said.

"Oh you missed the fascinating introduction to statistical abnormalities." Alexa rolled her dark brown eyes and shook her head. Small square glasses in a thin black frame perched on her nose. She had the most perfect olive skin and a mop of light brown hair, cut into a pixie style that accentuated the slimness of her neck. A few stray strands were stuck under her collar and Sebastian ached to reach out and free them, feeling the silky smoothness of her neck but he didn't dare. Tiny diamond earrings, a gift from her mother for high school graduation, so she'd told him, adorned her ears. She wore a pale yellow top with a matching pale yellow sweater and dark green Capri pants. Her books sat on her lap. She'd crossed her legs, letting one sandal dangle off the edge of her foot. She was short enough to sit comfortably in these narrow rows, which meant she wasn't a freak like him.

"Good thing I stopped reading," he said. "I don't know if my heart could take the strain."

She laughed, a musical sound that carried up into the air and set his heart pounding the way an economics textbook never would.

If only he had the guts to tell her.

At the front of the lecture hall, Professor Wilson tapped the bell on the side of his wood lectern, signalling the beginning of class.

"Thank you all for being on time today," he said. "I believe this is a record for this class." He seemed to stare pointedly up the room, right at Sebastian.

"Now let's review chapters seven to nine from last night. Please open your books…"

Alexa leaned over to Sebastian and made a soft snoring sound.

Sebastian flipped his book open, ducking his head down so Wilson wouldn't see the smirk on his face.

Then he noticed his shirt.

A stain of ketchup right above the second button.

The world hated him.

———∞———

"I think he's competing for world's most boring teacher," Alexa said as she and Sebastian streamed out of class at ten.

"Isn't that one of the Pulitzer categories?" Sebastian said.

He hugged his text book up to his chest, hiding the ketchup stain. For most of the class, he'd sat hunched in a weird Quasimodo posture, trying to hide the stain but now the text book helped cover the evidence of his complete inability to eat without spilling. Fortunately, Alexa didn't give him a second glance, which seemed to be the usual with her. Since meeting her in first year, he'd managed to hang out with her often, only to realize he'd somehow passed into the dreaded "friend" category. He'd been trying to find a way out ever since.

Of course, asking her for a date might be a start.

And why not today? Here they were walking along the path in the parkette between Osmere's Hall and the Edson Building, the weather unseasonably warm for this early April day. Newly budding leaves gave meager shade from the sunshine but Alexa lifted her face up, a slight smile on her lips as she closed her eyes to the light. Sebastian stumbled a little over his own feet watching her. Can't even look at her and walk at the same time, he thought with disgust. Sometimes he really was the most pathetic creature.

"This is perfect weather," Alexa said. She opened her eyes again and smiled at him. Sebastian felt all self-loathing drain away until the light of her smile.

"Yeah, it's great," he said. Great conversationalist, can't you come up with something else?

"I hope it stays this warm for the party at Delta Ki tonight. You're going, aren't you? The engineers are throwing it."

He remembered hearing vague rumblings around classes over the past week. Charlie, his connection to all and sundry parties had been talking about it for days.

"I'd heard," he said. "I was thinking about going."

"You should, it's going to be great."

He nodded. "I don't have class tomorrow until eleven."

"There, you can come and even stay late. No trying to rush to get to a class like Prof Wilson's." She chuckled and bumped him with her elbow. He stumbled but quickly righted himself. Just what he needed, to fall on his ass in front of her. You'd think that reaching his final height at eleven he'd be more coordinated but no.

"What time does it start?" he said.

"Nine. Of course, the cool kids won't get there til eleven which means I'll be there for ten." She laughed.

"Sounds like the cool kids will be late," he said.

Her smile widened. "Thanks, Sebastian."

A warm glow spread over his face and through his chest. His shoulders straightened. Sure, she was just being nice but maybe, just maybe, he could ask her to go to the party with him then it wouldn't so much be a date but could be and it might take the pressure off if they didn't have to go anywhere alone but had other people around and if it totally sucked, she'd have an out without having to completely destroy him...

"Hey guys!" Charlie's voice called from behind them. Steps thudded on the path as Charlie ran up. He burst between them, throwing arms around their shoulders.

"What's up?" Charlie's blond mass of hair managed to look uncombed and styled at the same time. He wore ragged jeans and a black t-shirt. He chewed with his mouth open but no matter what never seemed to spill anything on his clothes. A worn blue backpack hung on his left shoulder, although he never seemed to carry any books. Sebastian thought he was a science major, at least that's what he had said the last time they talked about it, but it seemed to change almost every month. He had the heavy lidded, slack faced look of a stoner but was vegetarian and never even smoked as far as Sebastian knew. Despite his occasional snoring to wake the dead, Charlie was a great roommate.

"We're just discussing the Delta Ki party," Alexa said.

"Oh yeah, that's gonna be great. You going?" Charlie said.

"Yes, I am."

"My man Seb and I are gonna be there." Charlie tightened his arm around Sebastian's neck. "What time you going? We'll met ya."

"Sure," Alexa said. "I'm thinking ten, ten-thirty."

"Sounds like a plan," Charlie said. "We can do that, right, Seb?"

"Sure," Sebastian said. "We can do that."

"Great." Alexa checked her cell phone. "I've got to head to class. See you tonight." She waved and veered off to the right, heading for the gothic castle-like shape of the Henderson Building.

As she disappeared over the rise and out of earshot, Sebastian pushed Charlie's arm off his shoulder.

"Thanks a lot, I was just about to ask her to that party."

"Yeah right, you were," Charlie said. "Like you've been just about to ask her a million times all year. Without me you wouldn't have seen her half the times you have."

"That's not true."

"It is so and you know it. Man, you got to grow a pair. You're lucky she hasn't been snatched up permanently. You have got to make a move."

"I was just about to."

"Right, right. So you make a move tonight. Nice party, a few drinks. She'll be mellow enough to say yes even to a dweeb like you."

"Thanks a lot."

Charlie grinned. "You know I only got your best interests at heart, man. But seriously, you have to ask her out. I can't take much more of your moping around after her. I'm gonna have to shoot you to put you out of your misery."

They started walking toward the Edson Building where Sebastian had class.

"I don't mope," he said.

"Oh yes you do."

"I do not!"

They argued all the way to class.

—⋈—

"You are not seriously changing again," Charlie said. "Are you sure you aren't a woman?"

"Shut up," Sebastian said. He shrugged out of the pale blue shirt. "This one has a stain on it."

"Everything you own has a stain on it." Charlie reached into the plastic packing bins that he used for his clothes. "Here, wear this. No stains guaranteed."

He tossed the plain black t-shirt at Sebastian, who caught it just before it hit the floor. He shrugged it on over his wiry torso. Although Charlie was bulkier than Sebastian, Sebastian's overall height gave him a slightly greater girth. The t-shirt stretched over his chest.

"It's a little tight," he said.

"Shows off your manly chest," Charlie said. "Besides, the black matches your hair. You want some gel for that?"

"I don't think it'll help." Sebastian swiped at his hair. It stuck out in all directions, even when he cut it short.

"Okay, you're done." Charlie switched out his daytime black t-shirt for a fresher black t-shirt.

"Hey, don't wear the same color," Sebastian said. "I don't want us looking like twins."

"Man, we so don't look like twins."

It was true. Even wearing similar clothing, they could not look more different. Sebastian stood tall with black unruly hair and a wiry torso, all gangly limbs and uncoordinated. Charlie was shorter with blond hair that looked styled even when not, a heavier build that bulked into muscle if he so much as looked at a weight, and who moved with the grace and agility of a cat.

Definitely not twins.

Charlie shook his head, his equivalent of combing his hair. Sure enough, his mass of hair settled into a perfectly casual style, guaranteed to draw the women at the party. Sebastian couldn't draw a woman to save his life. He relied on pity to carry him through. He only hoped Alexa Hammond was feeling some tonight.

"Ready, darling?" Charlie said.

Sebastian scooped up his wallet and jammed it into the back pocket of his jeans. "Ready."

They both retrieved jackets from the closet (worn leather for Sebastian, a torn jean jacket for Charlie) and they headed out.

The air had a chill to it, reminding Sebastian that winter might yet have another blast in her. Fortunately it wasn't cold enough to see his breath. He zipped his jacket and put his hands in his pockets. Charlie left his coat open, not seeming to feel the chill.

At night, the campus had a feeling of suspended animation, as if the busyness of the daytime hours got put on pause for the night, only to resume at the same spot in the morning. Sebastian inhaled the smell of the grass with the hint of decay beneath it. All the mulch and such from the fall had yet to be absorbed back into the ground but already he'd noticed various buds and bits of growth around.

The greenery around the campus was intent on spring.

They cut across a wide lawn, heading for Prospect Drive and the Delta Ki house. Even from several blocks away, Sebastian could feel the thumping of bass. In the distance, he saw a few other bodies heading in the same direction.

"Gonna be a blow out," Charlie said. He almost bounced beside Sebastian as they walked.

Sebastian nodded in agreement. Set inside a red-bricked, Victorian building that had been split into apartments, then renovated back into one main house with multiple bedrooms, Delta Ki was known for their parties. The End of First Semester one had lasted almost three days and only shut down when the students in the dorm had to leave for holidays. The End of Year party promised to be even bigger. Looked like they were warming up with this one, Sebastian thought. While he liked parties, even liked dancing a little, he wondered if he'd get a chance to talk to Alexa with so much noise tonight.

Stop it, he thought. There you go, being negative. Be positive for a change. Tonight you'll talk to her and she'll agree to go out with you. Just ask her.

He could do that. Yes, tonight he was going to do it.

He hoped.

The campus ground rose and curved in a gentle sweep down. On the right was a grove of trees with a concrete path running through it, the official path through this section of the campus although many just cut across the lawn. Occasionally, the campus put up signs to discourage walking through the lawn, protesting the erosion of the soil. It slowed the stream of students for a few days until someone stole the sign. Then the back and forth crossings continued.

If he'd been alone, Sebastian would have taken the path. He liked the feel of trees around him. It was comforting to be near something taller than him. He didn't feel like he had to slouch so much. But Charlie always cut across the lawn so Sebastian went with him.

As they drew closer to the street, the thumping increased, becoming actual sound that started to reverberate in Sebastian's chest. Charlie was practically jumping up and down now in excitement.

"Let's go, dude!"

He headed off in a jog, aiming for the second house on the left, a large old style Victorian with a huge porch and large bay windows on the first and second floors. Light illuminated the house, making it glow in the night. Charlie raced up the cobblestone walkway and disappeared inside, high-fiving people as he went. Sebastian followed in his wake, nodding at people as if he knew them. When in doubt, pretend you know what you're doing was Sebastian's philosophy.

He pretended a whole lot of the time.

Inside, the music hit him like a cricket bat to the face. Any possibility of conversation was lost, at least in this part of the house. Sebastian threaded his way down the hallway toward the back of the house, heading for the kitchen and possible drinks. Men and women crowded the living room as he passed. They swayed in a massive wave, reminding him of an old movie about bacteria absorbing other bacteria that he'd seen in elementary school. The hallway was no less crowded with people pressing together, mouths open in probable conversation but Sebastian couldn't hear any words over the pounding music.

Squeezing through a last group of four planted near the doorway, Sebastian popped into the kitchen. He caught a glimpse of Charlie in the old servants' stairwell, following a girl upward to the second floor. How he managed to zero in on women so fast, Sebastian never knew.

Even with the wall between, the music still thumped through the kitchen. Sebastian helped himself to a beer from the large wash bin filled with ice that sat on the old blue Formica table. He dug out a five and stuffed it into the donations box next to the tub.

As he twisted the top off, he felt a tug on his sleeve. He turned to find Wendell Morris standing beside him.

"Hey Sebastian," Wendell yelled, at least Sebastian thought he yelled it from the movement of his mouth.

"Hey Wendell," Sebastian yelled back.

Wendell leaned closer. "Did you read those chapters Wilson assigned last night? I can't believe he assigned five more!"

And they were off, discussing Wendell's discontent with the economics class.

Sebastian was almost halfway through his beer before he managed to disengage from Wendell. Making motions that he needed the bathroom, Sebastian headed deeper into the house. The front room on the second floor had been turned into a second living room. Several couches in hideous floral patterns or stripes in various stages of sagging sat around the room. The rest of the floor space near the walls was taken up by large, overstuffed pillows. Sebastian caught a glimpse of Charlie in the corner, sitting beside a pretty blond girl. He already had one arm around her and her hand rested on his knee. They looked to be in serious conversation mode.

Sebastian ducked out. He'd seen no sign of Alexa yet. He checked his cell phone. Ten forty-five, she should be here by now. Alexa was very punctual. That was one of the things he liked about her. She was reliable.

Maybe she'd come in while he was patrolling the upstairs. He headed for the stairs at the front of the house. Weaving his way down, he heard someone yell his name and looked over to see Tom from his business studies class waving. Angling that way, Sebastian glanced around the crowd. The hallway was even more packed but no sign of Alexa's light brown hair.

He ended up talking with Tom for another indeterminable amount of time as the party raged around them. The only indication of time passing was the occasional shift in tempo of the thumping of the music. Finally, Sebastian found his beer empty. He pointed to it and then back toward the stairs. Tom nodded, giving him leave to go.

Sebastian threaded his way toward the kitchen. Every thatch of brown hair caught his eye but none were Alexa. Had he missed her somehow? In this mass of people it wouldn't be difficult. He dumped his bottle and grabbed another. If he was smart he'd just take two; he didn't feel like drinking himself into a stupor tonight. He wanted to stay sharp.

Tonight he was going to do it. He was going to ask Alexa out.

The timing felt right. Maybe not so much the place with the pounding music and the hordes of people, but he could probably manoeuvre her outside, maybe into the backyard under the stars. It would be quiet and romantic. He could picture her face turned up toward him. Maybe he wouldn't even slouch. He'd stand tall, claiming his full height, and ask her out for dinner.

Yes, tonight he was going to do it, even if the thought did make him sick to his stomach.

Another patrol of the house. His cell phone told him it was now just after midnight, she had to be here by now and he'd just missed her in the throng. He'd spent way too much time talking to Tom. Now he was on a mission.

He took a big swallow of his beer and headed off.

First he covered the main floor, even poking his head into the living room cum dancing area and watched the crowd jump and shuffle and shake. No Alexa.

No Alexa in the packed dining room or kitchen, nor in the library that had turned into the impromptu smoking room, windows open wide and people hanging out with cigarettes in their hands. At least someone had thought to turn a fan on to blow the smoke out the windows.

He retreated from the doorway as a waft of smoke drifted out.

Okay, first floor, no sign of her. That left the second floor and the third floor, which was really a half floor. He pushed his way up the back stairs, using the black iron railing to guide him past two girls who slipped by, arms raised with beer bottles in their hands. Just don't spill on him. His head turned to watch the short skirt of the blond one as she bounced down the stairs.

His foot missed one of the wooden steps, making him stumble.

Good one, Sebastian.

Most of the bedrooms still had their doors open with people crowded onto beds or floors, drinking and yelling at each other over the music. Nothing.

Then he caught a glimpse of brown hair. Through the din, he heard the musical sparkle of her laugh. There she was in one of the side bedrooms, leaning against the wall with a guy just a couple of inches taller. He had his arm around her waist and as he leaned over to whisper in her ear, Alexa smiled. No, he wasn't just whispering, he was nuzzling her ear. And still she smiled.

And her hand came up to pull him closer.

All the air in the hallway vanished. Sebastian felt his stomach compress. His body folded in on itself. The beer bottle slipped in his fingers. He was only vaguely aware of it although his fingers clenched, holding the bottle tighter. He watched as she laughed again at something the guy said. And she smiled, nodding.

Smiled the way she never smiled at him.

No more, he couldn't watch any more. Even as her head began to swing around and her smile broadened at the sight of Sebastian and her hand lifted in a wave, he turned away. His feet stumbled to the wide, curving stairway at the front of the house. He blundered past people crowding the whitewashed steps. Somehow he lost his beer bottle in between the stairs and door. He thought he heard someone call his name but he ignored it.

It wouldn't be her, not when she was nuzzling some other guy.

The silence exploded around him as he burst out of the house. It seemed to roar in his ears as he hurried across the street, aiming for the path home. His long legs ate up the space, carrying him farther and farther away but not far enough to escape his own thoughts.

What an idiot he'd been. How could he think that a girl like that would be interested in a geeky guy like him? That muscly surfer type was more to her liking. Hadn't he seen it with Charlie all year? The guy practically only had to show up and inhale and the girls were all over him. Sebastian was still trying to figure out how to say hello. It had been like that his whole life. He was always left behind.

His feet hit grass and before he realized it, he was cutting across the lawn, taking the short cut, instead of the path. Whatever, what did it matter? He preferred the darkness of the lawn to the lit path. At least here no one could see his humiliation.

Part of him wondered if maybe he should have stayed and tried to talk to her but how could he after seeing what he had? He couldn't pretend that seeing her laughing and smiling like that at that guy hadn't cut into him. Hadn't he been watching it all year? Hadn't he been supportive when she'd been dating that idiot Chris?

Of course he had and that was the problem right there. He was always supportive. He was the *friend* and she'd never, never see him as anything else.

He was doomed.

And it was his own damned fault because he couldn't figure out any other way to get close to girls. He didn't have Charlie's ability to chat them up. The only thing he knew how to do was be nice. And when he was nice all they thought of him was nice.

Doomed to be nice.

Dammit!

He kicked at some dead leaves on the ground. His pace slowed. There weren't any leaves on the lawn. He lifted his head and actually looked around. In the gloom, he saw the suggestion of trees all around him. Somehow he'd wandered off the lawn and into the trees off the path. Great, that would be great to get lost in the trees until the sun came up. He still had class tomorrow even if it was later in the morning.

Well, he'd probably walked straight in so he would just turn around and walk straight out again. He spun and headed back. Without his head down, he felt the lower branches brush at the top of his head, messing his hair even more than usual. What did it matter? No one ever bothered to look at him twice so who cared?

Great, now he'd turned into a self pitying whiner.

Someone just shoot him.

He caught a suggestion of movement out of the corner of his eye to the right. Before he could turn, something slammed into him. He stumbled, his legs buckled with the force of it. He landed on his side, his arm pinned under his body. He tried to push up on the ground, his hand sinking into wet, squishy vegetation, but something dark fell over him. He smelled a sour stench. Something grabbed his head and yanked it to the side. A soft wetness licked along his neck then sharp pain pierced his skin. His body jerked and flailed. Something encased him in a vice grip, preventing him from moving. Soon he didn't want to. Ice seemed to flow into his body from his neck, paralyzing his muscles. Was this what snakes did, he wondered but there couldn't be any snakes here, not one this big. He tried one last time to kick his feet, thought he might feel a running shoe slip off and go spinning into the darkness. Then the pain didn't matter any more, in fact it wasn't pain at all, it was euphoria spreading through his limbs, leaving him weak and jelly-like and the vice grip was a warm blanket, wrapped around him by his mother. He could almost feel her kiss on his neck.

But her teeth... Oh her teeth were too sharp...

CHAPTER TWO

Voices called to Sebastian from the distance. He tried to turn away. He didn't want to get up, didn't want to go to school. Mommy, please send them away, but don't bite, no more…

The voices grew more distinct, separating into individual sounds then into individual words.

"Hey buddy, are you okay?"

"Don't touch him, I think he's hurt."

"What is that? Is it blood?"

The words pounded against Sebastian's skull. He tried to turn his head away from them but the stab of pain in his neck made him gasp, causing a flurry of voices around him.

"Hey, he moved! He's still alive!"

"My phone is toast. Call 9-1-1."

"The campus clinic isn't too far from here."

"Should we move him? Guy looks pretty messed up."

Sebastian tried to open his eyes but the lids felt like they have been glued shut. He was so tired, right down to his bones, to the cuticles in his nails, the pads of his toes. No one had ever been so tired and these guys were keeping him awake.

Keeping him here.

Where was here?

The question stirred his curiosity and with it any chance of sliding back into the inviting nothingness. Again he tried to open his eyes and this time was rewarded with a slight crack. Shadows loomed over him, coalescing into three men kneeling around him.

"Hey buddy, can you hear me?" said one near his head. "What happened to you? Was it a dog?"

"You really think a dog did this?" another voice said.

"Coulda been going for his throat," said the first one. "Look at the blood."

Sebastian's eyes managed to fight their way open. Pale light shone through the trees but it was enough for him to see by. The images of the men around him sharpened. The one at his head was slim with brown hair and a fashionable three days growth of beard. He wore jeans and a brown t-shirt that had been washed recently, possibly in the last few days. Sebastian could still smell the fabric softener.

The one crouching at his feet was stocky with a slight wheeze to his breathing. He wore jeans and a dark blue hoodie, neither of which had been washed within the past week and the hoodie needed it.

The final guy stood to Sebastian's side, shifting from side to side as he fumbled with a cell phone. Sebastian could smell the stink of stress staining his shirt under his jacket.

"Take it easy," said brown t-shirt guy. "We're gonna call 9-1-1."

"I can't. I told you my phone was toast." Nervous guy held out his phone as proof.

"We can't leave him here," said brown t-shirt guy.

"The campus clinic. It's just down past Oswell Hall," said hoodie guy. "We can carry him that far."

"Maybe we shouldn't move him." Nervous guy bit his lip as he shoved his useless cell phone back in his pocket. "If you guys didn't always leave your phones in the room."

"Don't start that again. Let's take him to the clinic." Hoodie guy extended his hands toward Sebastian's legs. Sebastian's gaze fastened on the guy's thick forearm. The skin hung a little loose, perfect for biting into and tearing out. Biting hard enough would ensure hitting the big vein leading to the wrist and flood his mouth with blood.

What?

What the hell was he thinking? He hated blood. Couldn't stand the sight of it. It always made him faint.

Sebastian tried to sit up but found his body wouldn't respond to his commands. A weariness settled thicker than any weights on his limbs. But he managed to lift his head. In the dim light, he saw the black t-shirt he'd borrowed from Charlie. Strange how it seemed to extend past his waist over his jeans. No, wait, the t-shirt was tucked in. What was that darkness on his legs? He blinked and the light seemed to sharpen, deepening the colors.

Was that… was that blood?

Sebastian's eyes rolled up and he fell back on the ground.

The next time he opened his eyes the light seemed blinding. He squinted and waited as his now-watering eyes adjusted. The first thing he noticed was the yellowing ceiling above his head. The forest canopy had never looked like that. He turned his head to the left, feeling something pull on the right side of his neck. It took a moment for him to get his hand working. It didn't seem to want to connect with his body. Finally he lifted his right hand, flexing the fingers to touch his neck. He felt a bandage. His fingers traced it along the side of his neck around the back and partway around the front. He remembered voices, disjointed. They blurred in with the party. Right, he'd been at the party last night. Memory trickled back. People, music, Alexa.

Alexa with that guy…

Now it wasn't just his neck that ached.

He felt the sides of the cot and pushed himself up. Sitting made the room spin a little. He took a deep breath, waiting for it to steady. There now. The walls steadied. Old white paint covered the walls of the long, narrow room. At the end, a window covered with dark navy curtains sat closed, but he could smell car fumes through it. The old stain on the door had yellowed, giving the brown wood an odd, sickly look.

A moment later, footsteps sounded from outside the small room. A woman in a white dress appeared in the doorway.

"Ah, you're awake," she said. She stepped forward. He caught a whiff of her perfume, weakened by time, just a trace of floral scent now. She touched his forehead, her fingers smooth. She then took his wrist, counting out his heartbeat.

"What happened?" he said. His throat felt raw making his voice come out ragged and croaking.

"I'm not sure," she said, still focused on the stainless steel watch on her wrist. Sebastian could hear the ticking of it, giving a slight echo in his head. "Three boys found you in the woods and brought you here. They said it was a dog attack."

Dog attack? He didn't remember any dog. But he didn't remember much about the woods either. He'd left the party, he remembered that now very clearly, after seeing Alexa and that guy cuddling. He'd been heading back to his dorm room. He'd walked across the lawn then...

Nothing.

He couldn't remember anything until the voices. Had he heard a dog? He couldn't remember.

"My neck?"

"Nasty abrasion," the nurse said. She looked up from her watch and released his wrist, laying it down in his lap. "I want you to keep the bandage on for a couple of days. Try not to get it wet. Be careful in the shower. Come back Monday and I'll take a look at it again. You were lucky those boys came along. It could have been a lot worse if that dog had gotten a good grip."

"Yeah," he said. "Lucky.

"I'll give you some antibiotics," she said. "I want you to go back to your room and rest. Are you in one of the dorms?"

He tried to nod but pain radiated up his neck into his jaw, making him wince. The nurse took his arm and helped him off the cot. For a moment, his legs felt like they didn't want to hold him but then the trembling muscles steadied. He kept one hand on the cot as he straightened. The faded black and white tile floor tilted a little then settled down. He took a couple of deep breaths and felt some strength returning with each one.

"I'm sorry I can't keep you here," the nurse said. She headed for the door, glancing back to make sure he followed. Sebastian took a tentative step. His legs held, his balance remained. So far so good. Another step and he felt more secure.

"I'm not set up to have people stay for more than an hour or two." She led him back into the front room. He smelled old paint and the stale scent of body odor. Four old blue fabric chairs lined the wall beside the door. A small desk sat opposite the door, facing two filing cabinets. He noticed flecks of paint peeling of the top corner of the cabinets, as if they'd been moved and bumped together, scraping the paint.

At the desk, the nurse opened a file and scribbled on a page. The scratching of the pen sounded loud in the silence of the room, although as he listened he realized it wasn't all that silent. He could hear the hum of the air being pushed in through the vents near the ceiling. From outside, he heard distant early morning traffic.

"What time is it?" he said.

"Just after six," the nurse said. She finished writing and set the pen down. She tore off a sheet of paper and handed it and a small bottle to him.

"This is enough antibiotics for the weekend," she said. "Don't bother trying to sell them or anything. There's no high at all. Come back on Monday and after I check your bandage, I'll give you the rest of the dose."

"Thanks," he said.

"And here's your wallet. I got your student information out of it."

He took his wallet from her and slid it back into his pants pocket. He stuffed the paper and pills into another pocket. He could feel the nurse watching him expectantly. He gave her a brief smile and then headed for the door. Each step still seemed slow but at least he didn't feel like he was going to fall over any more. His leather jacket hung on one of the pegs by the door. He pulled it down and slipped it on, his movements slow like an old man. As he shrugged it up his shoulders, the bandage on his neck tightened, sending a twinge of pain down across his shoulder. He winced but was facing away from the nurse so she wouldn't see. He didn't want her to notice and make him stay.

He grabbed the door handle and pulled the door open. The effort tired him and he waited a moment before moving through. The nurse didn't say anything. He could tell she just wanted him to leave.

Outside, the brightness of the morning sun stabbed into his eyes. He squinted against it, putting his head down. Too bright, way too bright. He tried to hurry, shuffling his feet against the pavement. The scrape of each of his shoes reverberated in his brain. He could feel a headache start to pound in his temples. It was from the sun, it was way too bright. He'd never had migraines before but he'd heard that light could affect them. Maybe he was having one now.

The light seemed to pour into his eyes, even as they narrowed into slits, sending pain shooting through his temples, over the top of his head and down his neck. Under the bandages, his wound throbbed in time with his heartbeat. All he wanted to do was lie down in a dark room and sleep. He still had a few hours before class. He could get more sleep.

He knew he'd feel much better after a rest, not so weak. His stomach churned and growled. He felt hungry but didn't want to eat. Along with the hunger, he felt sick to his stomach. He thought he remembered seeing blood last night. That always upset his stomach. He couldn't stand the sight of blood. It made him nauseous and he always fainted. His mother had wanted him to be a doctor but with his aversion to the sight of blood, even the tiniest drop, there was no way. Much safer to go into business. At least the only bloodletting there was metaphorical.

He cut across the street, not really paying attention to where he was walking. His feet seemed to know the way home, the way a dog would. He trusted them to get him there. Already he could see the lawn stretching out ahead of him. A slight dusting of frost sparkled in the morning sun. His breath hung in the chill of the air but he didn't feel cold. He hadn't even really noticed the temperature. The chill didn't permeate his leather jacket although he could feel the fabric of his jeans crackle in the morning air.

The frosted grass crunched under his feet as he reached the lawn. A breeze ruffled his hair, blowing from the direction of the trees, carrying the tangy scent of new leaves. The ground beneath him had a moist, dewy smell, thick and earthy as it absorbed the moisture from the frost.

The blare of a truck horn shattered the morning. He started, glancing around. No sign of a truck on any of the roads around him, not on the avenue he'd crossed or the one he was heading toward. It must be on the main road but that was on the other side of the campus.

Fatigue and his pounding headache stopped him from thinking more about it. He just wanted to get back to his room and fall into bed. Make sure the drapes were closed tight and pull the blanket over his head.

Finally, he reached the Saggon Dorm. Trudging up the steps to the door seemed to take the last of his energy. No way was he going to climb the five floors to his room. He'd take the ancient, decrepit elevator instead.

But as the door swung shut behind him and he passed into the darkened lobby of the building, he felt his headache start to recede. The skin across his scalp loosened. He opened his eyes wide. Tension drained from his neck and shoulders. Even the wound hurt less.

Must be really tired. Before he thought about it, he headed for the stairs like he always did. Dimness filled the stairwell but he could see the worn blue markings on the edge of the stairs, the plain metal railing that lined the wall, even the dull beige paint that peeled up near the ceiling.

He started up the stairs, gaining more energy with every step until by the fourth floor, he was bounding upward. Strange. He still felt tired but a weird energy seemed to pulse through him in the darkened stairwell. He reached the fifth floor and let himself into his room.

To the left, Charlie lay sprawled across his bed, arms and legs flailed out, hanging over the edges. The dorm single bed could not contain him. Sebastian crept across the room to the window separating their beds. Sunlight still leaked around the edges of the drawn drapes. He tucked them around the window, trying to block out as much of the light as possible. The fabric resisted his efforts. Dammit.

He turned away, rummaging in his desk drawer, and digging out some scotch tape. A few well-placed strips of tape held the drapes tight across the edges of the window.

There, that was better. Not as dark as he would prefer but better than before.

He dropped the tape back into the drawer and started pulling his clothes off. Unlike Charlie who dropped his clothes all over the floor (on his side of the room), Sebastian normally hung his up or at least draped them over the end of the bed to be put away later, but he was too tired for that. He dropped them where he stood, leaving a pile of clothes beside his bed. He crawled under the blanket and pulled it over his head. In the darkness, he felt the wound on his neck tingle. He knew he should set his alarms for class but he was too tired to move again. Crossing the lawn in the morning had taken all his energy.

Later.

He'd do it later.

As sleep began to take him, he thought briefly about the clothes on the floor. Charlie was going to think he'd begun to rub off on Sebastian, especially after lending him the black t-shirt.

His last thought before sleep claimed him was: *hope I didn't get any blood on it.*

Then he slipped into darkness.

～

Comforting darkness surrounded him when he opened his eyes. Something pressed against his face. His blanket. He still had the bed sheets pulled up over his head. He stretched, feeling his bones crack and his muscles shift. He pulled the sheets down, narrowing his eyes in case the light was too bright again.

Shadows still filled the room. Across from him, Charlie's bed now sat, messy, but empty.

Strange, Charlie didn't have a class until early afternoon today.

He sat up and stretched his arms over his head. The bandage pulled on his neck. He knew he shouldn't pick at it but he felt an almost overwhelming urge to scratch at it. Forget about it, get ready for class.

The extra sleep had helped. He felt more energized. Stepping out of bed, his body felt coiled and ready. He grabbed his robe off the hook on the back of the door. Slipping it on, he took his towel and headed out for the bathroom.

An unusual silence filled the dorm hallway. Had everyone decided to skip their Friday classes? Maybe after the Delta Ki party, they'd all decided to sleep in. Sebastian didn't do that too often. His grades would suffer if he didn't attend class regularly and his parents had shelled out a lot of money for this education, as they so often reminded him.

In the shower, he remembered the nurse reminding him not to get the bandage wet. That meant washing his hair was out of the question.

He settled for running a wet comb through it.

In the mirror, his face looked pale with dark circles under his hazel eyes. His black hair slicked back on his head, different from the usual mass of wildness, made him looked like an old time gangster. The wad of bandage on his neck made it look like another head was starting to sprout. The itchiness started again and with it, the desire to rip the bandage from his neck. His hands lifted and curled around the edges before he realized what he was doing. Stop that, he knew better. He didn't want to get an infection or anything. Besides that close to his head it might head straight to his brain. He wasn't sure if that was how infections worked but why risk it?

He towelled off and wrapped his robe around him. His body felt odd, energized and sluggish at the same time. How much had he drunk at the party last night? Three, maybe four beers, certainly not enough for a hangover. It was probably residual trauma from the dog attack.

If it was a dog attack.

A niggling doubt lingered in his mind. Why couldn't he remember? He'd had dogs jump at him before but never as high as his neck. Even when he was a kid he recalled his neighbor's beagle Baxter had jumped at him when he cut through their backyard on the way home. Baxter's leap had only brought him up to Sebastian's butt. He'd ended up with quite a tear in his pants that day. His mom always wondered what happened to those pants.

So a dog leaping as high as his neck seemed... odd. But what else could it be? The urge to remove the bandage again tried to overwhelm him. Instead, he went back to his room through the still empty hallways.

Where was everyone?

He was just out of sorts, he decided, as he closed the door behind him. Everything seemed weird today because of the dog bite. Maybe he should skip his classes and stay in bed. Recovering from an attack was certainly a good excuse.

But if he skipped class he wouldn't see Alexa. The thought of her brought the flood of memories from the party. That was right, she'd been all over that guy in the side bedroom. She'd smiled and laughed at him the way she never did with Sebastian. That was when he'd left the party. That was the reason for the dog attack.

Or whatever it was.

So why would he care about seeing her today? She obviously had no interest in him, since she was all over surfer guy. Sebastian had spent the past few years mooning over her and she never even noticed.

Why couldn't he just quit?

He tore off his robe and threw it on the bed. Digging out clothes gave him an excuse not to think, but the question reverberated in his head, demanding to be answered.

Why couldn't he just quit? Why couldn't he just quit?

He pulled on jeans and a pale blue shirt. As he tucked the shirt into the jeans, he glanced down. Of course, naturally.

A mustard stain.

Screw it. He wasn't going to change. Mustard stain be damned.

His resolve lasted a second before, with a curse, he striped the shirt off and dug out another. This one he inspected before slipping it on. A light green that brought out his eyes, his mother had said in her letter when she sent it. He'd only worn it once.

Now twice.

Why did he care about a mustard stain? For the same reason he knew he couldn't quit. He was hopelessly (yes, admit it, it was hopeless) in love with Alexa. And, dammit, even seeing her nuzzling up to that guy last night hadn't changed it for him.

Dammit.

He stuffed his wallet and cell phone into his jeans pockets then grabbed his backpack. After making sure he had the texts and notebooks for the day's classes, he slung it onto his shoulders. He felt his back muscles flex under the bag. Funny, it seemed lighter today, easier to carry. He pulled it off his shoulder and checked the contents again. Yep, he had all the texts, each one seeming to weight five pounds on its own. Strange. He slung it back on his shoulders. Still felt lighter.

Maybe he was finally getting used to carrying everything.

He headed for the stairs and reached the bottom in no time. As he crossed the lobby, he saw bright sunshine streaming through the front door window. His pace slowed. It seemed to take forever to reach the door, then he pushed it open and was through, stepping out onto the front step.

The sunlight seemed blindingly bright. He squinted against it. A headache started almost immediately, pounding in his temples as he headed off. Five steps and he regretted not bringing his sunglasses. Ten steps and his legs began to slow down. Energy drained from his body. He'd never felt so sluggish so quickly before. What was wrong? Even his thoughts seemed lethargic in his brain, hampered by the pain lacing over his skull. Residual reaction from the attack? He'd never be able to sit in class like this.

He made it to a nearby tree and sagged against the trunk. The light covering of new leaves gave a brief respite from the blazing sun. As he rested in the shade, he pulled out his cell phone. Turning it on, he stared at the numbers showing that time. That couldn't be right, he thought. He was on his way to his late morning class. How could it be after five in the afternoon?

How could he have slept all day?

He'd never done that, not even when he was sick. His body seemed unable to sleep during daylight hours. Or it least it had been that way before.

It was the bite or the injury or whatever it was, obviously he'd needed more recovery time than he'd anticipated and it seemed he needed more now. All the energy he'd felt upon waking had evaporated. His head throbbed with pain. The bright sunshine stabbed into his eyes, even with the protection of the shade under the tree. He couldn't go to class like this, no way.

He took a deep breath and pushed away from the tree. The door to his building looked miles away even though he'd barely walked fifty feet. He trudged away from the tree. As soon as he left its slight shade the sun stabbed down at him again. He could feel it burning on his skin, cooking his flesh. Crazy thoughts, it was early April, the sun couldn't possibly be that hot, but the impression endured.

His shoulders hunched against the light. Under the bandage, his neck started to itch, making him want to tear the bandage off. His hands clenched into fists, his nails digging into his palms.

A few more steps, just a few more steps.

His heart hammered in his chest. The echo of it reverberated in his head, making each stab of pain pierce deeper and deeper into his temples. The sun blazed down on the back of his head. He felt it burning through his hair to his scalp. Much more of this and he thought he would burst into flames.

His foot hit the concrete step. It was important, this step, he knew he was supposed to do something about it but he didn't know what. With his head bowed, he started at the grey concrete, noting the small imperfections in it, tiny dents and discolorations. How could he have not seen those before?

That didn't matter, but he couldn't remember what did matter. It was so bright, so terribly bright. His eyes wanted to close. His head lifted. He saw the door in front of him and the darkness of the hall beyond.

Yes, darkness. That was why the step was important, it led him to darkness. Cool, dim, safe darkness. It was right there, through that door.

All he had to do was take the first step.

Lifting his left foot took all his strength. He rested with his foot on the step and his hands on his knee. Just a few more steps and he would be inside, in the dark, in the coolness, safe from the raging sun.

He tried to draw in a deep breath but his lungs felt constricted, like a vice had wrapped around them and was squeezing. A wave of dizziness swept across him from his head down to his feet. His stomach lurched. He felt nauseous.

He opened his mouth, trying to suck in more air. With a massive effort, he lifted his other foot onto the step. Leaning forward gave him the momentum to move forward. He hit the door and leaned on it. The click of the door lock sounded like an explosion in his head. The door swung open. His feet stumbled as he tried to follow it in. He staggered over the door jam and reached the wall, sliding down it as the door swung closed, blocking out the sun.

He sat in the shadows with his eyes closed. The wound on his neck itched incessantly but he didn't have the strength to lift his hands to it. His skin felt like it had been on fire, the worst sun-burn anyone had ever gotten. But as he sat in the dim hallway, the feeling eased. The vice around his lungs loosened and he could draw in a deep breath. That in turn helped reduce the throbbing pain piercing his temples and clenching his scalp. Each breath released the pressure until he could open his eyes again.

Well, obviously trying to go to class had been a big mistake. He needed more recovery time than he'd thought. A lot more.

After a few minutes, he felt strong enough to stand. When he reached the elevator, energy seemed to flow into his limbs. By the time he reached his room, still cloaked in darkness, he felt normal.

He dumped his backpack on the floor and sat on his bed.

What had happened out there? He wanted to tell himself he just needed more rest, more recovery from the attack last night. It would be easy to say it and if he said it often enough he knew he might even come to believe it.

But it would be a lie.

And he knew it.

He glanced over at the window, where he'd taped the drapes along the edges so the light wouldn't get in. He'd done it so it would be dark enough to sleep, at least that's what he'd thought when he'd pulled out the tape but now he knew the truth.

He was afraid of the sun.

CHAPTER THREE

Charlie returned to the room just before seven. Sebastian heard his footsteps coming down the hall from the direction of the elevator. He recognized the shuffling, sliding pace of his friend before Charlie even reached the door. The hinges creaked and Charlie stood in the doorway.

"Hey, why's it so dark in here?"

He hit the light switch. The ceiling light clicked on, flooding the room with light. Sitting on his bed by the window with his back against the wall, Sebastian winced as the light came on. He waited to see if the pain in his head would start, the feeling of burning on his skin, or the suffocating pressure in his chest but nothing happened. He'd been afraid to turn on the light. Several tests of pushing the drapes back and letting the late afternoon sun shine on him had shown he was indeed susceptible to it.

He hadn't wanted to test the light bulbs.

Charlie tilted his head at Sebastian. He tossed his backpack onto his bed.

"Dude, where've you been? What happened to your neck?"

"I got attacked last night," Sebastian said.

Charlie had sat down on his bed and was pulling off his running shoes. He dropped them on the floor.

"What? You okay?"

"I... I don't know. I thought I was."

"Whadya mean? You need a doctor? Let's go." Charlie shoved his feet back in his shoes and headed for the door.

"No, I can't," Sebastian said. "The sun..."

"What about the sun?"

Sebastian looked at the drapes, hanging so innocently. He clenched his hands on his lap to stop them from trembling.

"I can't go out in the sun."

Charlie frowned. "What?"

"It hurts," Sebastian said. "I'm allergic or something."

"Allergic? Since when?"

"Since today. I tried to go out. It..."

The words clogged his throat. He couldn't explain the intensity of the pain, of the fatigue, of the outright *aversion* he felt for sunlight now. It scared him. He'd never had such a strong reaction to anything and every time he thought of it, his neck itched. His neck with the bandage covering the wound that he couldn't remember getting, couldn't remember what gave it to him. A dog, he kept telling himself, but he couldn't remember any dog. A vague suspicion hovered in the back of his mind but he refused to give it any more thought because it was too ridiculous, too insane, too... terrifying.

Still frowning, Charlie stepped toward the bed. "Okay, no doctor then. So what happened to you?"

Sebastian drew in a shuddering breath. "I left the party early, I don't know maybe around midnight. Something like that. I was walking back here and somehow ended up in the trees off the path. Got turned around or something. I turned around to come out and something hit me."

Charlie grabbed the desk chair and straddled it. He gripped the back and leaned forward. "You were mugged?"

"No, I still had my wallet. I don't know what it was."

"What? What do you mean 'what?'"

"Whatever it was did something to my neck. The nurse said she thought it was a dog bite or something."

"Nurse? Where'd the nurse come from?"

"I woke up in the clinic," Sebastian said. "Some guys found me and took me there. That's what she said. I think I might have seen them."

"Do you know who they were?"

Sebastian shook his head.

"Maybe we should find out," Charlie said. "Maybe they saw something."

Sebastian glanced over at the window. "Let's wait for the sun to go down."

Charlie sighed. "Okay, whatever you say. I'm going to grab something in the cafeteria. You want anything?"

Sebastian shook his head. "I'm not hungry."

"I'll be right back." Charlie stood up, pushing the desk chair away, and walked to the door. He turned back and frowned at Sebastian before he left. Sebastian could smell the concern rolling off his friend as the door clicked shut.

Wait, that was weird. He could smell concern. Sebastian breathed in deeply through his nose. How could he do that? How did he even know what 'concern' smelled like? The air had a kind of bitter scent, overlaying Charlie`s usual musk smell, and when was it that he noticed Charlie's smell?

He jumped off the bed and paced the room.

What was happening to him? He was afraid to know but he had to, had to find out, had to find a way to deal with it. He paused near the door. Maybe he should go down to the cafeteria and get something to eat but he'd told Charlie the truth. He wasn't hungry.

Now that he thought of it, that was strange too. He hadn't eaten anything since dinner the night before. The last thing he'd had was the beer at the party. He hadn't eaten all day and yet he didn't feel the slightest bit hungry.

Anxiety, a reaction to what had happened to him, all of it conspired to drive away his appetite.

Maybe if he repeated that to himself often enough, he'd believe it.

He turned away from the door and walked over to the window. His hands clenched at his sides. He wanted to move the drapes aside, see if the sun was down. Something inside him told him it wasn't quite gone yet. A few more minutes left before the sun had fully disappeared from the sky. But he couldn't *know* that. How could he?

Standing just out of the way, he peeled the drapes aside and peered out.

Long shadows covered the street outside. Sunlight still brightened the sky, blazing on the sides of the buildings facing it. A few clouds in the sky glowed on the bottom, reflecting sunlight. The sunlight, even as weak as it was, made him squint. He could feel the throbbing begin in his temples. He released the drapes and let the fabric fall back into place.

An allergy, please let it be an allergy.

He tried to ignore the itching at his neck.

A final glance behind the drapes confirmed Sebastian's thought that the sun had finally gone down. He'd known even before he pulled the fabric aside but he had to check, just to be sure. But he had known it, had felt it in the way his anxiety drained away and how his body felt more energized, more than it ever had before. He put on his shoes and slipped on his leather jacket, then stood waiting for Charlie, practically vibrating with suppressed energy. He heard Charlie coming down the hall and opened the door.

"I'm ready," he said.

"Okay." Charlie gestured past him. "Let me get my coat."

Sebastian moved aside, letting Charlie enter. Charlie gave him an odd look over his shoulder as he reached for his jeans jacket lying at the foot of his bed.

"What?" Sebastian said.

"You seem weird," Charlie said.

"I'm fine," Sebastian said. "Let's just go to the clinic. I want to talk to those guys."

"Sure." Charlie slipped on his jeans jacket. "Let's go."

They headed down the hallway toward the elevator. Sebastian found himself noticing the worn pattern in the carpeting, the flaws in the paint on the walls, how some of it peeled near the ceiling or looked faded as if there weren't enough coats to cover the plaster. The faint aroma of food drifted up from the cafeteria but wasn't enough to mask the scent of all the people living on this floor.

"Did you talk to Alexa?" Charlie said as they rode the elevator down.

Alexa. Her name brought a twinge of pain and regret to Sebastian's mind. He shook his head.

"No," he said. "I didn't get the chance."

"You should have," Charlie said. "She was looking for you. Maybe if you hadn't left so early."

The unspoken comment hung between them: maybe if he hadn't left early this, whatever it was, never would have happened.

Like it was his fault.

"She seemed kind of preoccupied." Sebastian spat out the words and then regretted it. He didn't want to talk about it but Charlie was already turning toward him.

"I thought you didn't see her."

"I said I didn't get the chance to talk to her."

"Okay, what happened?" Charlie said. From his tone, Sebastian knew his friend wouldn't be put off. Dammit, he never should have said anything.

Sebastian shook his head. "It was nothing."

"Screw nothing. Spill already."

"I saw her with some guy. They looked pretty cozy."

"And you didn't bother to talk to her." Now Charlie shook his head. "Sebastian, sometimes you're an idiot."

They reached the front door. Sebastian pushed it opened and stepped outside. The last rays of sunshine faded from the sky. Even with the streetlights, the shadows deepened toward night. A soft breeze blew across the street, rustling the leaves of the trees in the distance. He heard the hiss of the grass and dust scraping against the asphalt.

Charlie followed as he headed toward the clinic. "So who was this guy?"

"Just some guy," Sebastian said. He didn't want to think about it, didn't want to remember how Alexa had laughed and smiled at him, the way she never did at Sebastian.

"She was looking for you," Charlie said.

"You said that," Sebastian said.

"Even today she was wondering why you weren't in class, she asked me about it."

Sebastian shrugged. Sure, she asked. He was her *friend*, why wouldn't she ask? That was the sort of thoughtful person she was, she asked if she didn't see you. She was nice that way. It was one of the things he liked best about her.

Dammit.

"Can we just deal with one thing at a time?" Sebastian said.

"Okay, okay," Charlie said.

They continued on, crossing the lawn and heading for the street. Sebastian listened to the whisper of the breeze in the trees. Every breath he took brought him different smells: the decaying leaves, the new buds on the trees, the moist ground, the asphalt, even the lingering smells of students walking the path, a mix of sweat, deodorant, hairspray and laundry detergent.

By the time they reached the clinic, Sebastian marvelled at how smoothly his muscles seemed to flow as he moved. His normal gawky walk had changed to a gliding motion that ate up the ground and used minimal energy. His legs had always felt almost too long for his body but now they moved in an easy coordination with his arms and torso. Several times Charlie had had to ask him to slow down until they arrived at the clinic. Charlie grabbed onto the side wall, gulping in air.

"What's the rush, dude?" he said between puffs.

"I wasn't rushing," Sebastian said. His skin tingled. "You okay?"

"Yeah, let's go in."

Sebastian opened the door and walked into the clinic. He recognized the small waiting area. A row of chairs lined the window, facing into the room. One guy holding his arm glanced up then back down at the magazine he was leafing through. No one else was in the room. The desk at the far end stood empty.

"Is the nurse here?" Sebastian said.

"She's with someone," the guy with the magazine said. "I'm next."

"Should we sit down?" Charlie said.

Sebastian looked over at the desk. He remembered her making notes in a file on that desk, a file that probably had all the details of his attack. He wanted to look for it but the guy`s presence inhibited him. Otherwise, he imagined ransacking the room looking for the file.

The image shook him. What the hell was he thinking? He didn't do stuff like that. He saw Charlie staring, jerking his head at the chairs. Sebastian nodded and followed. They sat down. He could still feel Charlie's gaze on him and knew his friend was frowning again. He could smell the bitter scent of concern.

Five minutes later, the nurse shuffled in from the back room. She stopped as Sebastian stood up.

It wasn't the same nurse. He should have known that.

The other guy struggled to his feet, still holding his arm close to his body. "I was next," he said.

"I just need to ask a question," Sebastian said. "I was here last night. Some guys brought me. I just need to know who they were."

"I don't think I can help you," the nurse said. She was younger than the one from this morning. She smelled of talcum powder.

"That's right, she can't help you because I'm next," the guy said.

Sebastian ignored him. "If I could just look at my file," he said. "Sebastian Lockhart."

The nurse shook her head. "I'm sorry, I can't let you look at that. It's privileged medical information."

"But it's information about him," Charlie said.

"I'm sorry, I can't let you look at the file," she said.

"Please," Sebastian said. "I really need to see that file." He stared at her, thinking, come on, come on. She opened her mouth to refuse him again, he could feel it in the way her mouth almost formed the words. Then her jaw slackened. The talcum powder smell grew slightly sour. Her eyes got a far away look.

"Just a peek," he said.

"Just a peek," she repeated.

She turned away from him and then walked in a jerking fashion toward the desk. Sebastian followed.

"What the hell?" he heard Charlie murmur behind him.

"Hey, I was next," the guy said.

"Shut up," Charlie said.

The guy sat back down on the chair, holding his arm in his lap, and muttered to himself.

The nurse pulled open a drawer and withdrew several files. She flipped through them then placed one on the desk. Sebastian saw his name in black marker along the top. He opened the file.

He flipped past the identification page, glanced at the recording of the injury (deep abrasions, minor blood loss, neck trauma), reviewed the symptoms observed by the nurse (patient presented unconscious, symptoms of shock) and finally came to a list of the men who had brought him in. He grabbed a sticky note and a pen from the desk and scribbled down the names, Jeff Lanson, David Clark and Morris Hildebrandt, roommates at Branson Hall, returning from the bar. He closed the file, not wanting to see the description of the injury again but the words burned in his mind.

Abrasions, blood loss, trauma.

"Thanks," he said to the nurse. She blinked at him.

He placed the pen on top of the file and turned to Charlie. "Let's go."

Charlie followed him out of the clinic. "You get the names? Where to now?"

Sebastian waved the sticky note. "Branson Hall."

⸎

They retraced their steps past their dorm and headed north to Branson Hall, one block north and then two streets over. Charlie reviewed the note and then handed it back to Sebastian as they walked.

"I don't know these guys," he said.

"You know someone at Branson?" Sebastian said.

"Sure, Barry at Branson," Charlie said.

"You know someone everywhere."

"You would too if you actually talked to people instead of, you know, walking away."

He was talking about Alexa, Sebastian knew, but he wasn't going to be drawn into that conversation.

"I want to talk to these guys."

"Whatever," Charlie said.

They continued on in silence. Around him, Sebastian listened to the cacophony of the night. New and rich smells filled every breath. Where was this all coming from? How had he not been aware of this before? It almost made him dizzy except somehow his body seemed to be able to process it all. He didn't want to think about that too much, just like he didn't want to think about Alexa. Just find these three guys and see what they could tell him.

One step at a time.

Despite its old style name, Branson Hall was a large concrete rectangular box, even more industrial looking than their own dorm. Wide concrete steps led up to two double doors. They pushed through and found themselves in a large front foyer. A desk stood off to the side with a security guard sitting behind it.

"Can I help you?" he said.

"We're looking for some students who live here," Charlie said. He gestured at Sebastian who pulled out the sticky note.

Charlie read off the names.

"I saw them leave earlier," the guard said. "They didn't say where they were going but it's a good chance they went to the Grady's Bar."

Charlie nodded, handing the note back to Sebastian. "I know where that is."

As they headed down the concrete steps, Sebastian said, "Grady's Bar, I don't know that one."

"It's a sports bar," Charlie said. "Lots of jocks hang out there."

Sebastian let Charlie lead the way but soon he could tell where the bar lay. He could smell a hint of nachos and beer on the air, underlying the thicker scent of sweat. By the time they reached the double oak doors, Sebastian was almost able to identify twenty different scents inside.

It kind of unnerved him.

A roar went through the crowd as they stepped inside. Some game blared from the television set over the bar. Sebastian ignored it, scanning the patrons in the room.

"Let's ask at the bar," Charlie said. "I bet they're here often enough that the bartender knows them."

"Wait." Sebastian grabbed the sleeve of his friend's jeans jacket. "I think that's them in the corner." He pointed across the bar.

Charlie squinted through the dimness. "You sure? I thought you said you hadn't seen them."

"I might have," Sebastian said. "I'm not positive. Let's just check, then we can ask the bartender."

He moved forward, not waiting for Charlie's reply. It seemed so strange for him to take control like this, push ahead without full agreement. He was the original 'let's reach a consensus' guy, the 'let's review all the angles' guy, but here he was, just jumping in. It felt strange and exhilarating at the same time.

What the hell was going on with him?

As he reached the table, the three men sitting there looked up. He noticed recognition dawn on each of their faces.

"Excuse me," Sebastian said. "Are you Jeff Lanson, David Clark and Morris Hildebrandt?"

"Yeah," said the slim one with brown hair. "You're that guy we found in the park."

"I'm Sebastian Lockhart, this is my friend Charlie. I was just wondering if I could ask you some questions?"

David nodded. "Sure, grab some chairs."

They pulled a couple of chairs from the nearby tables and sat down. A waitress appeared at Charlie's elbow, pen poised over pad.

"Two beers," Charlie ordered.

She nodded and walked away.

"You okay?" asked the stocky one that sat across from Sebastian.

"Yeah," said Sebastian. "I wanted to thank you guys for taking me to the clinic. I really appreciate it."

"Any time," said the stocky one. The others nodded and raised their glasses in a salute before taking a drink.

The waitress returned, depositing two beer glasses in front of them. She hovered between them. Charlie picked up his glass and took a sip. That was his cue, Sebastian realized. He pulled out his wallet and paid the girl, motioning around the table to order a round for the three guys. She nodded, plucking the money from his hand and walked away.

"Sorry we couldn't call 911," said the stocky one. "Jeff's phone died. That's why we had to take you to the clinic."

The third guy, Jeff, shrugged as he sipped his beer. "Yeah sorry. My battery is crap."

"It all worked out," Sebastian said. "But like I said, I have a few questions."

"Sure," David said. "Shoot."

Before he could speak, the waitress returned again with three additional beers. She set them down and Sebastian paid her. Morris, the stocky one, smiled and raised his still half full glass beside his new one.

"Any time you want to get mugged again, we'll be there to help," he said.

"That's what I wanted to ask you," Sebastian said. "Did you guys see anything? See what happened? Who attacked me?"

The three looked at each other and one by one shook their heads. "No." "Sorry." "Nothing," sounded from all three but Sebastian smelled an acrid odor arising from one of them. What did that smell mean? It took him a moment to realize one of them was lying.

"Anything?" he said. "A shadow maybe? Even if you don't think it's important. Please think back."

Both David and Morris looked thoughtful but Jeff glanced down at his beer, his fingers sliding up and down the glass wet with condensation. That was where the acrid smell was coming from, Sebastian realized, the other side of Charlie, from Jeff.

Did that mean he'd seen something? If so, why wouldn't he say? Sebastian took a deeper breath and under the acrid smell he smelled something else. A sour, pungent scent.

Fear.

"We were coming home from the bar," Morris said. "I didn't see anything."

David shook his head. "Me neither. I practically fell over top of you before I saw you."

Jeff took a sip of his beer. He swallowed and shook his head.

"You sure?" Sebastian said. He looked directly at Jeff.

"Yeah, I'm sure."

"You don't seem so sure," Charlie said.

He'd caught it too, Sebastian thought. It wasn't just me.

Jeff's fingers tightened on his beer glass. "Of course I'm sure."

"You just seem a little nervous," Charlie said. "That's all." He glanced around the table. "Sure you were just walking home?"

"What the hell does that mean?" Morris said.

Sebastian put a hand on Charlie's arm. "Easy," he said. "I think I remember you guys. I really just want to know what you saw. I don't remember anything else from last night. Every little bit would help." He directed the last line at Jeff.

"Jeff, did you see something?" David said.

"No, I couldn't," Jeff said. "How could I? It was dark."

"There were lights on the path," Sebastian said.

"Yeah but you weren't on the path," Jeff said. "You were in the trees."

"And why were you guys there?"

Now they all shifted in their chairs. Morris's shoulders twitched in a shrug.

Finally David sighed. "Look they aren't cops," he said to the others. He turned to Sebastian. "We'd heard someone had planted marijuana in the trees."

Charlie choked on a mouthful of beer. He grabbed a napkin and coughed into it. Sebastian pounded his back until he stopped coughing. Finally Charlie wiped his mouth and dropped the napkin to the table.

"That's a total myth," he said. "Seniors make that up to get the first years riled up. I can't believe you fell for that."

"Well, it might have been there," Morris said.

"Right, like campus security wouldn't have found it by now."

"They might not of!"

Charlie shook his head.

"I don't care why you were there," Sebastian said. "I just want to know what you saw." He looked over at Jeff. "I think you saw something."

"I didn't." Jeff tried to straighten with indignation but his white fingers clutching his glass gave him away.

"Come on, Jeff," David said. "Just tell him what you saw."

"Okay, okay." Jeff took another pull from his beer and set the glass down on the table. He pushed the empty glass away and grabbed the fresh one.

"We were looking for the plants," he said. "You guys were up ahead." He moved his chin to indicate Morris and David. "I was just lagging behind. I heard someone cry out. There was this shape hunched over you."

"What kind of shape?" Charlie said. "A dog?"

Jeff shook his head. He took another drink. "Too big to be a dog. I don't know. It was kind of hunched over him. It sort of looked like a person."

"What?" Morris said.

"I'm just saying what it looked like," Jeff said. "I didn't say it was. Maybe it was a really big dog. I don't know."

Sebastian felt as if his stomach was dropping out through the bottom of his feet. He grabbed his own beer and took a long drink. It slid down cold but the taste was flat, bland, as if the beer was off. He set the glass down half finished.

"That's all I wanted to know," he said. "Thanks." He stood up.

"Oh really?" Charlie glanced up at him and then back to his almost full glass of beer. He raised it to his lips and gulped down over half the contents. Putting the glass down, he wiped his mouth on the back of his hand. "Cheers, guys."

"Cheers." "Cheers." They called after them, raising their glasses. Sebastian had already turned away, heading back toward the entrance. The flood of noise and smells assaulted him again; this time it downright terrified him. What the hell was going on? He pushed through the crowd faster and faster even as he heard Charlie calling for him to wait up.

He finally burst through the front door, stopping five paces down the sidewalk. The cool, fresh air filled his lungs as he breathed in. He bent over, hands on his knees, taking deep breaths to calm his pounding heart. He heard Charlie burst through the door after him and stop at his side.

"Sebastian, what the hell is going on?"

"I don't know," Sebastian said. "I think... I don't know." He shook his head. He couldn't form the words that kept trying to coalesce in his head. It was just too insane.

"Come on," Charlie said. "You knew that guy saw something. Are you remembering who attacked you? Who was it?"

"I don't know!" Sebastian said.

"Don't give me that. You're a crappy liar. Spill."

Sebastian shook his head. No, it was crazy. Everything was crazy, from the moment he'd left the party and walked home, getting lost in those trees. Why the hell had he turned into those trees?

"Come on!" Charlie said.

"All right," Sebastian said. "I think it was a vampire!"

CHAPTER FOUR

Charlie took a step back as Sebastian stood up.

"A vampire," Charlie said.

Sebastian spread out his hands. "What else could it be?"

"You're kidding, right? 'What else could it be?' Like there's no other explanation that's rational? Did it ever occur to you it was a guy with a dog? He sics the dog on you and then tries to mug you. The three guys scare him away. That's rational."

"What about my reaction to the sun?" Sebastian said.

"You're in shock," Charlie said. "It was a traumatic experience. You've always been a bit of a pussy, Sebastian."

Sebastian frowned. Maybe he wasn't the most coordinated, confident guy around but he didn't think he was a pussy.

"Don't give me that hurt look," Charlie said.

"I am not giving you a hurt look."

"Oh yes you are, your little feelings are hurt. Poor baby."

He knew what Charlie was trying to do, distract him from what they'd been talking about, as if that would make it better. He shook his head.

"I want to take a look in the trees."

Charlie threw up his hands. "Of course! Shall I bring a stake while we're at it?"

"Just shut up," Sebastian said. "Are you coming or not?"

"Lead on, Christopher."

"Christopher?"

"Christopher Lee. He was Dracula in the Hammer movies."

"I know that," Sebastian said. "I'm not Dracula."

"But if it was a vampire," Charlie said. "You could be eyeing my blood right now." He took a sharp intake of breath and covered his neck with his hands.

"I'm gone." Sebastian turned and started down the street, heading for the park and the trees.

He never should have said anything, never should have spoken the word aloud and risked ridicule. Charlie would never let him live this down now.

And why would he? It was ridiculous. How could Sebastian even consider it? His footsteps slowed. Maybe he'd been working too hard and this attack was a final push. Maybe something inside him had snapped, grabbing onto the trappings of the attack to create something fanciful from it. A way to escape his dreary regular life of mundane classes and pathetic social life. If he was a vampire, he wouldn't have to deal with any of that.

He stopped and turned back to where Charlie stood watching him.

"It is crazy, isn't it?" he said. "I don't feel crazy."

Charlie walked up to him and put a hand on his shoulder. "Maybe you're just tired."

Sebastian nodded. "I do feel tired."

"Of course you do, it's been a hell of a day. Let's go home."

Charlie led him back to the dorm. As they walked through the lawn section, Sebastian glanced over at the path and the trees beyond but he didn't say anything. He knew Charlie wouldn't want to look.

Sleep didn't come that night. Sebastian lay on his bed staring up at the ceiling. Beside him across the room, he listened to Charlie's deep breathing, coming out in the occasional snore. He'd found soon as he lay down that if he shut his eyes and concentrated, he could hear the guys on the other side of the wall. They both had a snorting type of snore that sounded off rhythm from each other. Another set of noises that he thought came from below had a distinct wheeze to them, as if the breathers were stuffed up.

He shouldn't be able to hear them. He'd never heard them before. The dorm was well constructed with concrete. Even blaring music had a hard time getting through yet he heard the snorts and snores as if they were in the room with him.

He sighed. Just sleep, but he couldn't. He felt wide awake and energized. Lying here in bed just made him antsy.

Getting dressed in the dark was easier than he thought it would be. He tried not to notice how clearly he saw everything, how it all just looked in deeper shades of grey. His night vision had never been that good before. But he'd been lying in the dark for a while. His eyes had adjusted.

Maybe if he repeated that often enough, he'd believe it.

Sure, because it was rational to think he'd been attacked by a vampire.

He slipped out of the room and closed the door with a soft click. Through the door, he listened to Charlie's breathing; no change. He knew he would have heard it if there was any difference.

The thought made him shiver a little.

He headed for the front of the building. So was he going to keep up the pretense with himself that he wasn't going to check out the trees? No, he had to be at least honest with himself. He had to look, had to know if there was anything there to give credence to his theory. If not, then maybe he could relax and let it go.

And if there was some evidence there?

One step at a time.

The night air tasted cool and fresh as he stepped outside. He inhaled deeply. Smells flooded him, the grass, the ground, decaying leaves, dog manure, the asphalt, tree pollen, the brick and concrete from the building, but most of all the musk of people. Now less obvious than in the building, he realized he'd been smelling people all around him. Each one had a slightly different odor, a mix of sweat and skin and cologne and hair product. When had that to come to him?

He pushed the thought away. The trees, he was just going to check out the trees. Once he saw that there was nothing, he could go back to bed and maybe deal with the fact that he was losing his mind. That had to be it, just like Charlie, in not so many words, meant. It had to be. Maybe Sebastian just needed a break. Maybe this school year had been too much for him. He didn't think it had; sure the classes were a challenge, trying to keep on top of all the assignments, but he was doing it. He had a few friends. Alexa... well, okay maybe that was a challenge but he didn't think he was losing it.

But would he?

He stepped onto the grass and headed for the path.

Beneath his feet, he felt the grass crunch and flatten with each step. The crack of the blades released new and subtle bursts of aroma. He heard a dog bark in the distance, the echo of its bark sounding far away. Occasional traffic noise came to him but there were no cars driving on campus. Again the noise sounded distant.

His body tensed as his anxiety level rose. He shouldn't be able to hear or smell any of this stuff, never mind how well he was seeing in the dark. As he approached the path, he could easily distinguish the trees on the other side, even this far from the nearest light. He could see the rough texture of the trunks, the shading and deepening shadows, the way the new buds perched on the branches.

How could he do that?

Relax, he thought. Just relax. Take a look in the trees, see what's there and deal with it afterward. He took a deep breath. His thudding heart slowed.

He headed down the path, aiming for where he thought he'd turned into the trees. Then he paused. He hadn't thought to bring a flashlight. It seemed pretty stupid to head into the trees without one. How would he see anything?

He glanced back at his dorm. Did he want to go back and dig around the room, looking for a flashlight? Did they even have one? He thought Charlie had a penlight on his key chain, he could go back for that but he didn't want to. He wanted to go into the trees now. He'd waited long enough.

Something called to him in those trees.

He tried not to think about it as he stepped off the path and slipped between two trunks.

His hand brushed the side of one of the trees, feeling the rough texture against his palm. If he pressed hard enough, tiny fragments of bark would break off on his skin, but he didn't press. A light breeze rustled the leaves above his head. He tried to step carefully over the ground but each step brought him down on twigs and leaves which snapped and cracked under his weight, sounding as loud as gunshots to him. He inhaled the scent of them, tasting the richness of the leaves and the age of the trees. He'd never realized how much was inside here, how much life, how much energy. He could feel it flowing through the trees into the ground and back again.

He could feel it flowing through him.

His skin tingled with it. Each step brought it more into his awareness until he felt himself almost drunk with it. He veered toward the left. The energy led him that way and he followed until he found himself standing in a small empty spot.

On the ground, he noticed a large section of leaves and twigs crushed and bent as if something large had been there. This was where he'd fallen, he realized. The energy in the trees had led him here. He glanced around. He recognized the break in the bark on that tree there. He remembered the way the branch stuck out of that one over there. This was the spot, the spot where something... happened.

So, was there evidence here?

He bent down to search the ground. Hadn't he landed on his side here? His hands explored the area, almost feeling a suggestion of residual heat from his body, as if the ground remembered him. But he couldn't see anything. No trace of footsteps, no piece of fabric, no dropped weapon.

Just the flattened leaves where he'd fallen.

He closed his eyes. Could he remember anything more now that he was here? He'd only been walking through here a little more than twenty-four hours ago. Surely, some scrap of memory should come to mind.

He remembered being caught up thinking about Alexa. About Alexa with that guy. She'd never looked at Sebastian that way. He was always the good *friend*. He could even hear her saying how she wouldn't want to ruin their friendship.

The suppressed emotion he'd been avoiding welled up inside him. He could almost smell it seeping through his pores. Of course, why would she ever go out with him, an over-tall, geeky guy who couldn't keep from spilling food on himself and could barely hold a coherent conversation?

He'd been thinking all of that as he stumbled his way into the trees and it would have stank for miles, he realized.

And what would have smelled that?

He'd realized he was in the trees and turned to head back. Then... what? He tried to remember. Come on, think! His hands dug into the pile of leaves in front of him, scraping down to the ground. Something hit him. He'd fallen. Not a dog, bigger than a dog. He would have remembered a dog, remember the fur, the smell.

But he did remember a smell, a stench of something sour...

He remembered his head being yanked to the side and then... nothing. The memory dissipated. He slammed his hands down on the ground in frustration, flinging leaves and debris into the air. Why the hell couldn't he remember? It was just a stupid mugging, wasn't it?

Oh please, let that be what it was.

There was no answer here, nothing but the silence of the trees and his heart pounding in fear. Why was he afraid here? Residual fear from the attack or something else?

He didn't know.

He sat back on his heels and bowed his head. He lifted his hands from the ground, feeling the leaves and dirt trickle out of his palms. He rested his hands on his knees, getting ready to stand.

A twig snapped off to his left.

He froze. His head swung. More trees darkening in the distance into shadows. Through the leaves above he caught a glimpse of night sky. The light breeze waved the leaves at him but nothing to break a twig.

Nothing that wanted to be seen.

He focused in that direction. For a moment, it looked the same then the trees shifted, lightened, as if his eyes sharpened. He could make out more detail on the trunks, see the leaves scattered on the ground in irregular bunches. Had some of those bunches been disturbed just now?

How could he do this? The thought crossed his mind, making his hands tremble on his knees. His heart pounded. This was impossible, wasn't it? He couldn't just zoom in with his vision this way.

He listened, beyond the sound of his own thudding heart, and heard the whisper of the wind flitting through the trees. The buzz and chirp of insects grew louder. He heard footsteps on asphalt and realized they were coming from the street at the end of the path. The traffic in the distance rumbled louder.

Still nothing that would have snapped a twig.

Had he been mistaken? Maybe it was an animal or maybe he really was losing his mind. He closed his eyes, feeling tears press against his eyelids. He was tired, that was all. It had been a long couple of days. Charlie was right. He was just traumatized by this incident.

When he opened his eyes and stood up, he found that his sight and hearing had reverted to normal. Now it was just the usual high sensitivity instead of the ultra-close sensitivity.

That's enough, he thought. Time for bed. There were no answers here. Time to stop asking the question. Time to move on.

He left the trees and headed back toward his dorm, his hands stuffed into his pockets so he wouldn't scratch at his neck, which itched like crazy under his bandage.

~⌀~

Sebastian woke in the morning with his head aching. Even before he opened his eyes, he realized Charlie had thrown the drapes open wide, letting sunlight into the room. Sebastian jumped from the bed and dragged the drapes shut. As a darkened twilight filled the room, his headache lessened, settling into a dullness at the back of his head.

His mouth felt gummy. He crossed to the small fridge and opened it, pulling out the pitcher of water. He poured some into his glass and drank it. That helped and even eased his headache a little. He poured another glass and replaced the pitcher. He took the glass and sat back down on his bed.

Charlie's bed was empty. Sebastian checked the clock. Just after ten. He'd slept late for a Saturday. As he finished the glass of water, Charlie walked in, rubbing a towel through his wet hair.

"Morning," Charlie said.

Sebastian grunted.

"Aren't we cheery this morning?" Charlie said. "Why did you shut the drapes?"

"The light bothers me," Sebastian said. "Gives me a headache."

Charlie frowned. He crumpled the towel in his hands.

Before he could say anything Sebastian stood up. He grabbed his toiletry bag from the stand by his bed.

"I'll be right back," he said.

He headed for the bathroom down the hall. Fortunately it was empty. He was late for the early risers and early for the late risers. As he set the temperature in the shower, he hesitated before stepping in. The nurse had told him not the get the bandage wet. He wouldn't be able to let the water run over his scalp and he needed that right now.

Screw it, he thought. His fingers peeled back the medical tape. He yanked the bandage from his neck and tossed it at the garbage can. It hit the side and balanced on the edge. He left it and stepped into the shower.

The water flowing over his body eased the tension in his muscles. He hadn't even realized he was so tense. But the feeling of the sunlight beating on his skin... even the thought of it made him tighten up. He tilted his head back, letting the water pour over his hair. He felt it trickle down his neck and over his shoulders, chest and back. Soon the tightness drained away.

He gave himself an extra few minutes in the shower, then turned it off, reaching for a towel. He dried quickly and stepped out of the tub. Steam fogged the mirror. Sebastian swallowed and used a hand cloth to wipe the mirror.

His reflection looked back at him, paler than usual. His dark hair slicked back with water, revealed his neck. He leaned closer to the mirror and tilted his head.

He saw the abrasion, more like a tear in his neck. It had the puffy, whitish look of damaged flesh. Through the wound he could already see the new skin, all pink and tender-looking. For some reason, it looked thin, as if a single membrane of skin held his neck veins and muscles intact.

Any little trauma would cause a complete rupture.

He glanced over at the used bandage still balanced on the edge of the waste basket. Couldn't reuse that. He should have thought to bring a bandage from his room.

Draping a towel over his shoulders bunched it up around his neck, hiding the injury. He returned to his room. Charlie was half dressed, puffing his hair in the mirror beside the door. Sebastian was relieved to see he hadn't opened the drapes. He gave Charlie a grateful smile as he shut the door.

He rummaged in the desk and came up with several bandages. Tossing the towel onto his bed, he moved over to the mirror. Charlie shifted to give him room and looked at his neck.

"Yikes, that does look nasty," he said. "Good thing that dog didn't get a good grip."

Sebastian unpeeled a bandage and placed it over the wound. It covered half of it. He unpeeled the second bandage.

"Yeah," he said. "Good thing."

"See, it doesn't look like a vampire bite," Charlie said. "No real puncture wounds, it's just a tear."

Sebastian finished covering the wound. Now if he wore a collared shirt, the bandages would hardly be noticeable.

"Right," he said to Charlie.

A little half smile betrayed Charlie's relief. "Let's grab some breakfast downstairs."

"Sure."

Sebastian dressed, making sure to wear a collared shirt and long sleeves. Before they left the room, he grabbed a ball cap and his sunglasses.

The cafeteria had large windows.

The headache pinched his temples as they walked in. Sunlight streamed in through the floor to ceiling windows on the far wall, opposite the food line. Sebastian had always liked the windows because they faced out toward the lawn and the trees, but today with the sunlight streaming, he wished they were a solid wall.

He followed Charlie into the food line, grabbing a plastic tray from the pile at the end. With the sunlight throbbing at his head, he didn't pay attention to the food. Finally he followed Charlie into the seating area close to a wall.

Charlie sat first with his back to the window, forcing Sebastian to sit opposite. The headache settled into his temples and across the top of his scalp, a steady throbbing. At least it didn't seem as bad as yesterday, he thought. He hoped that was a good sign. Maybe tomorrow it would be even better.

He looked down at the food on his tray. He'd just copied whatever Charlie had taken: scrambled eggs, toast with jam, home fried potatoes, coffee and juice. The scent of the food bombarded him. He could smell the oiliness in the eggs, the bitterness of the coffee, the sickly sweetness of the strawberry jam. None of it appealed to him. He didn't even feel hungry.

He lifted the juice glass and sipped.

Across from him, Charlie dove into his food, shovelling a mix of eggs and potatoes into his mouth. He ate for a few minutes before he realized Sebastian wasn't eating.

He nodded at Sebastian. "Hey, aren't you eating?"

"I'm not really hungry," Sebastian said.

"You should eat something," Charlie said.

"Juice is fine."

Charlie frowned. He wiped his paper napkin across his mouth. "When'd you eat last?"

Sebastian shrugged. He knew exactly when but didn't really want to talk about it. Thursday at dinner, then the beer that night. Since then it had been a little water and now this juice.

"You eat yesterday?" Charlie said.

"I don't remember," Sebastian said. "I felt kind of out of it."

Charlie shoved his empty plate aside, pulling his coffee toward him. "Don't bullshit me, man. You don't wanna tell me, fine. But don't lie."

Sebastian heard the inflection of hurt in his friend's voice. "Sorry, I'm just really not that hungry."

"Fine. Don't eat it then." Charlie stood up. He grabbed Sebastian's tray and his own, carrying them over to the racks. He returned for his coffee but didn't sit down. Sebastian held his juice glass in front of him.

"Hey, I'm sorry."

"It's okay." Charlie sipped his coffee, his gaze moving past Sebastian. Through the medley of smells and sounds, Sebastian smelled a familiar floral scent wafting closer and heard a step nearby. Charlie held his coffee cup up to his face.

"Hey guys," Alexa said from over Sebastian's left shoulder.

"Hey Alexa," Charlie said. "I was just finishing. You can have my seat."

He turned and headed for the racks, carrying his coffee cup.

Alexa walked around the table and sat across from Sebastian. She looked clean and fresh, her brown hair shining with the sunlight behind it. A concerned half smile decorated her face.

"I didn't see you in class yesterday, Sebastian."

The pounding of his heart overtook the thudding of his headache. "I wasn't feeling well yesterday."

"I heard," she said. Her hands rested on the table in front of her. He could smell the polish on her fingernails even though they were dry.

"I heard you were mugged," she said.

Embarrassment heated his face. He glanced down at the half full juice glass in his hands.

"I don't remember much about it," he said.

"That's terrible," she said. "But you're okay now, right?" Her hand reached across and touched his free one. Her fingers felt silky smooth on his hand. He wished he could capture those fingers and hold them in his palm. Then the memory of her laughing with that guy from Thursday night rose up in his mind. There wasn't anything special going on here, he realized. She was just being a good friend.

"Yeah," he said, "I'm okay."

Her smile widened on her face. "That's good. I hate if anything really bad happened to you."

He smiled back. "Thanks. Did I miss anything yesterday?"

Her fingers slid away. He missed them immediately and wanted to grab her hand and hold on but he didn't move. Just let it go.

His heart ached in time with his head.

"Not much," she said. "Just more reading from Stevenson and Eldridge gave more details on the economic analysis he wants completed by end of term. I've got notes for you. Want to come get them?"

She stood up, standing beside the table. She wore a white shirt with a red sweater and jeans. Her feet were pushed into flat black shoes with a red bow on them. A small purse was slung over her shoulder.

Past her, Sebastian saw the brightness of the sun.

She wanted him to go out into that.

His stomach tightened. Even with only the juice, the thought of going out into the sun nauseated him a little. But she was looking at him expectantly. What could he do?

Maybe he could try it. His headache wasn't as bad today. Maybe he'd be okay in the sunlight. He pushed the glass away and stood up. His legs trembled a little but he forced them to steady. It'll be okay, he thought. Just a little walk. No big deal.

She smiled and headed for the door. He took a breath and followed. He pulled out the ball cap and slipped it on his head then pushed the sunglasses up on his face. As she opened the front door, letting light spill into the foyer, he found the glasses gave him some comforting dimness.

"You look like you're in disguise," she said and laughed.

He gave her a faint smile. "No autographs."

"Right, Mr. Celebrity, let's go."

She moved out of the cafeteria. He followed. He noticed Charlie sitting several tables over, sipping his coffee. His friend nodded.

He'd planned this, Sebastian realized. Probably called Alexa and told her everything, including his talk about a vampire. Dammit! He wanted to slap that coffee mug out of Charlie's hand. If he told Alexa, anyone could have overheard and it would be all over campus in no time. Great, just great. Sure, he'd like to be noticed but not like this, not for being mugged by a vampire.

Ahead of him, Alexa reached the front door and pushed. Sunlight glowed in the foyer, obvious even through his darkened lenses. The sight of it drove all concern about his image from his mind. Now he was only concerned about surviving the sunshine.

Alexa held the door open. She looked back at him.

"Are you coming?"

He tilted the brim of the cap a little farther down on his forehead. All or nothing now. He stepped forward, into the foyer, into the sunshine. He could almost feel the heat of it through his jeans and then his shirt but not as bad as yesterday.

Okay, that was okay.

Alexa released the door and stepped down off the stoop. "Don't worry, there's no one here for autographs."

Expecting the worst, he took a deep breath and stepped outside.

Heat from the sunshine beat down on his head. It increased his headache, making it throb stronger in his temples. His stomach tightened but he couldn't tell if it was from the light or from his anticipation. His limbs felt a little tingly but there wasn't the same level of weakness as yesterday.

Maybe it was okay. Maybe it really had just been shock, a reaction to what happened. Maybe his body overreacted and was slowly returning to normal.

His shoulders sagged with relief. A headache and slight tingling he could handle, not the overwhelming nausea and weakness. Maybe it just meant he couldn't stay out in the sun too long. Fair enough.

"Where did it happen?" Alexa said.

"In the trees off the path," Sebastian said. "I was coming home from the party."

She shuddered. "That's horrible. Right here on campus. Did you call the cops?"

Funny, it had never occurred to him. "No."

"Well, you should call them."

"I didn't see anything," he said. "Besides, they didn't take my wallet. The nurse thought it might have been a dog from the wound on my neck."

"Wound? You were wounded?" Alexa stopped walking. "Charlie didn't say anything about that."

Charlie, just like he'd thought. "I supposed he's been spreading it around," Sebastian said. "Makes a good story."

"He only told me," she said. "He's worried about you."

Sebastian rubbed at his left temple. His finger caught the arm of the sun glasses and shifted up, letting more light into his eyes. He winced, feeling them start to water. The throbbing in his head was worse.

"Yeah okay," he said. "Can we get inside? This sun is really bothering my head."

"Sure." She started walking again. In the bright sun, the cuffs of her white shirt beneath her sweater shone like beacons.

His heartbeat echoed in his ears then he realized the rhythm was slightly off. He touched his chest. His heartbeat was different from what he was listening to. He lengthened his stride, coming to Alexa's side. The beating sound got louder.

Her heart. He was hearing her heart beat.

How was that possible?

His hands started to shake. It wasn't just her heart beating that bothered him. His temples throbbed under the brightness of the sun. Out of the corner of his eye, he watched the side of her face, of her neck. He could almost feel the heat coming off her skin. He could smell the scent of her, a mix of floral perfume, hair gel, soap and fabric detergent and underneath it the warm, heady scent of her skin.

Of her blood.

He tasted saliva in his mouth.

"No!" He jumped away from her.

"Sebastian?" she said. "What's wrong?"

"I... I have to go." He turned and ran.

"Sebastian! Wait!"

Her voice faded in the distance as he ran. His legs pounded the ground. His arms pumped as he raced away. But it didn't matter.

It would never matter.

He would never be able to outrun himself.

CHAPTER FIVE

Sebastian spent the day in the main campus library, hiding in the coolness of the stacks. It was easy to lose himself in there. Huge rows of books, rising almost to the ceiling, filled the library's top six floors. The main floor held the check out area and tables for studying with a row of single booths along the front wall near the floor to ceiling windows. But from the second floor up, it was rows upon rows of bookshelves, cool and musty.

As he wandered the stacks, he became quite acquainted with the differing odors of the books. The latest ones smelled new with a sharp tang of glue underlying the crisp scent of the papers. The oldest ones had the deepest smell of mildew and rot. The remaining books ranged in smell from almost new to getting old, with drying paper.

Much to his surprise, he was able to get a lot of his reading work done. The library had a full collection of student textbooks for use, but not loan. He was able to hide away in the stacks with different textbooks throughout the day. He'd only missed Friday, only three classes. He read three chapters in every textbook just to be sure he covered everything.

That took him to almost five o'clock. On a Saturday, the library stayed open until nine. The sun would set around eight so he still had a few hours.

A few hours to distract himself and try not to wonder what the hell was wrong with him.

It was now almost two days since he'd eaten and he still didn't feel the least bit hungry. Not for food anyway. He tried not to think about it. Every time it came to mind, he'd grab a textbook and force himself to read several pages until the feeling disappeared. It was harder if someone was nearby. He could smell them among the books. At those times, he thought hiding in the library maybe wasn't the smartest idea with the enclosed space but he didn't want to face the sunlight yet. If people wandered too close, he fled to another floor. All the while the wound on his neck itched.

He tried to tell himself it was just healing.

He tried to tell himself he wasn't losing his mind.

He didn't believe either.

By now, he was sure Alexa probably thought he was mad, running away like a lunatic. Was there any chance less than zero with a girl? If so, he'd reached it for sure. No girl wanted to go out with a guy who was crazy. But he hadn't felt like he was going crazy before that attack on Thursday night. Had his brain maybe just been waiting for the right moment to snap? He'd seen other people at school buckle under the stress but that had been mostly in the first couple of years. Now in third year, most people were used to the pressure, had developed coping mechanisms to deal with it. He thought he had. Had he been deluding himself?

From the far end of the row he caught the scent of a person. He didn't want to see anyone. He hurried away toward the other end and then moved several rows over only to encounter someone else browsing the books. How much longer would he have to dodge people? He didn't want to keep doing this.

He'd left his cell phone in his room. An unintentional action but now he was glad for it. That meant Charlie or Alexa couldn't find him. If he'd had it he would have felt compelled to keep it on and then to answer it if they called. Now he didn't have to do it. He knew they'd be angry, wondering what the hell was going on with him. If he could answer that, he'd tell them. But first he had to figure it out for himself.

Each floor had a clock hanging between the two elevators. It was always risky chancing it near the elevators, more opportunity to be too close to people, but he had to risk it. He had to know if it was late enough to leave. As he stepped out from the row farthest to the right of the elevator, one female student stood in front of the elevators, arms full of books. She turned her head toward him, her blond ponytail swishing across her back. Rimless glasses were pushed up her nose. She smiled at the sight of him.

"Hey Sebastian, how's it going?"

It took him a moment to remember her name. "Hi Brigit," he said.

"I didn't see you in stats Friday," she said. "Smart move. Stadler was more boring than usual." She rolled her eyes, her head following the movement away from him, exposing the curve of her neck. Her body shifted. He caught the scent of her, sweet and musky, over the thicker scent of paper in her hands.

He swallowed.

His mouth felt dry.

The clock. He was supposed to be looking at the clock. He wrenched his gaze from her and started at the wall, his gaze searching and finally settling on the white clock face. Black arms pointed but he couldn't read the numbers.

The scent of her flooded his brain.

"I don't think it should be a mandatory class," Brigit said. "Some of the kids are protesting."

Even in the cool air, he felt himself start to sweat. His heart pounded. He tried to breathe shallowly, tried not to draw too much of her scent in but he couldn't help it. It surrounded him. She smelled so warm, so enticing...

So delicious.

"I think I forgot a book."

He spun and stumbled back along the nearest stack. Rows of books blurred beside him as he ran. Halfway toward the back of the row the scent of her finally dropped away. He breathed in the smell of glue and paper. He sagged against a shelf of leather bound history texts and closed his eyes. Thank god for the books and their smell, thank god.

"It isn't going to help."

He jumped at the sound of the voice. Several books teetered on the shelf and fell, hitting the floor with a loud thump. Pages fluttered open. At the end of the row, a woman stood leaning against the shelf with her arms folded. Dark brown hair was pulled back from her face and hung in a pony tail over her shoulder. She cocked one eyebrow at him.

"You going to pick those up?"

"Uh, yeah." He bent to grab the books, trying to keep his eyes off her. The one book slipped and wouldn't close. He finally managed to grab it and stuff it back onto the shelf, not even paying attention to if it was in the right order.

Even as he fumbled, she stood still with an almost preternatural calm as she leaned against the shelf. If he couldn't see her, he would never have known she was there. She didn't make any sound and he couldn't smell her. After a couple of days of smelling everyone it startled him not to be able to smell her.

"Do you realize what's happening to you?" she said.

He shoved the last book into place and wiped his hands on his pants. "What do you mean?"

Her head jerked at him. "The sunlight, the enhanced senses. Have you eaten anything since it happened?"

"Since what? Who are you?" he said.

"Just answer the question," she said. "Have you eaten since Thursday night?"

Why would she ask that? "I'm not hungry."

She frowned. "You have to eat. Not eating can tip the balance. It hasn't got a firm foothold in you yet. You need to eat something."

She stepped away from the shelf and slid a backpack she'd been wearing off her shoulders. She set the pack down and unzipped it. The pack was worn tan leather, well used from the look of it. She pulled out a granola bar and held it out to him.

"Eat this," she said.

He hesitated to take it. Who was this girl? She didn't look like a student. Although she was young, she had a hardness to her. She wore olive pants and a beige shirt with a black vest. The clothes looked almost as worn as the pack, the colors softened and faded with use.

Her hand pushed the granola bar closer to him. "Take it!"

Her tone was so insistent he snatched the bar from her hand. She lifted the pack back onto her shoulders.

"Now unwrap it and eat it," she said.

He still hesitated.

"Don't make me stuff it down your throat."

From the look on her face he knew she'd do it. Although she was a full head shorter than he she had a look of determination that he'd be foolish to ignore. He unwrapped the bar and took a bite.

It tasted bland and flavorless. He chewed it. The texture was like cardboard.

"I know, it's gross," she said. "All food is now. Unfortunately that doesn't improve. You just have to get used to it. Now swallow."

He did so, feeling the lump of chewed granola bar sliding down his throat. It felt unnatural.

"You have to keep eating," she said. "It's crucial during this time. Your body is still adjusting, still fighting the infection. Once you're reached your equilibrium you can relax but right now you have to be vigilant. You can't let it get the upper hand or you'll be lost."

"What are you talking about?" he said.

"I think you know," she said. "Have you been smelling their blood yet?"

His mouth paused open in front of the granola bar. How could she know?

She nodded. "It usually happens a couple of days after. If you're smelling it today, you're a bit early which means it a farther along than I thought. You'll have to be extra careful. Keep eating."

He bit down on the bar and chewed.

"Who *are* you?" The words sounded mumbled around the bar as he chewed. It really did taste disgusting.

She hooked her thumbs into the straps of the backpack and leaned back against the wall. "I'm Jessica," she said. "I'm like you."

He swallowed the food. His stomach grumbled as if in protest. "What do you mean you're like me?"

"You're what, eighteen?" she said.

He straightened with indignation. "Twenty. Twenty one next month."

"I was nineteen when they got me. The symptoms took longer to manifest but they did. Sunlight sensitivity, enhanced senses, smelling the blood of the people around you. It always smells wonderful, that doesn't go away either. You just have to stay away from it and remember to eat occasionally. Food that is."

He shook his head. This girl was crazy. He didn't understand what she was talking about and he didn't know why he was even bothering to stand here listening to her.

"Keep eating," she said.

He took another bite. Now his stomach rumbled louder, objecting to the granola bar. He didn't blame it, the thing was really disgusting, bland and cardboardy. It grit against his gums and felt like mush on his tongue. Why the hell was he eating this crap? His stomach gurgled. A wave of nausea spread up his torso. He spit the mouthful of bar back into the wrapper.

"This is gross," he said. "I'm not eating this."

"You have to." She straightened from the shelf and took a step toward him. "Are you okay?"

His stomach clenched, protesting the granola bar. He doubled over. The remaining bar fell from his hand. Pain radiated from his stomach through his body. He stumbled back hitting the shelf behind him. Books teetered and fell. He was dimly aware of some of them striking his back but it was a minor irritation compared to the agonizing twisting of his stomach.

He dropped to his knees. His heart was pounding, galloping at a furious rate. He was going to vomit. He didn't want to, not in the library but he could feel it happening, his stomach rebelling against the bar he'd eaten. It was probably bad, stale. He should have known better than to take something from a woman he didn't know. She'd poisoned him!

He felt hands on his shoulder and forehead. Cool fingers pressed on his temples, massaged points on his head. The rebellion in his stomach eased. He still tasted bile in the back of his throat but it didn't have the urgency of coming out. Instead, he felt the nausea settle. His heart rate slowed, easing as the pressure from the fingers lessened. Finally, he felt just one hand on his shoulder.

"You're worse than I thought." Her voice sounded in his ear. "It must have gotten close to turning you."

He opened his mouth. It tasted sour and gummy. His lips were dry.

"What are you talking about?"

"The vampire, of course," she said. "You know that's what bit you, right?"

He turned his head to her. From this close, he caught a whiff of the scent of her shampoo but still nothing from her. She was still a blank to him, as if she didn't exist. Then he saw the side of her neck, partially hidden by the collar of her shirt, a paler patch of skin, gnarled and knotted like scar tissue.

It looked like a bite mark.

Kind of like his.

He pushed away from her. This was crazy. There were no such things as vampires. It was one thing for him to say it to Charlie. Charlie would tell him he was nuts and then he could buy into that. It was stress, school stress, stress over Alexa, whatever, but it couldn't really be a vampire.

Vampires didn't exist!

"It's okay," she said. "I freaked out for quite a while myself. But I had a lot more time than you do. You can't afford to freak out now, not while it's still working away in your system."

"What do you mean?" His voice sounded weak, shaky.

"I think of it like an infection," she said. "Some of the others get all mystical or spiritual. Whatever. I think it acts more like an infection. You've been exposed and your body is currently fighting but you need to support it if you're going to win."

"Then I'll get better?" he said.

"One step at a time," she said. "Let's get you out of here and some place where you can get some decent food. And this time you're going to eat it all even if you feel like throwing up."

She took his arm and helped him to his feet.

"How did you know I felt like throwing up?"

"I felt that same way the first time I had to eat," she said. "Actually the first few times, but then it goes away. It's still not great fun but at least I can do it without heaving now."

She began to steer him toward the elevators.

"Where are we going?" he said.

"I've got a little place," she said.

≈

Much to his relief, night had fallen by the time they left the library. He relaxed more in the gathering twilight. Jessica looked even more formidable out here in the dusk. Her expression brightened and her eyes reflected any spec of light. Her lips twisted in a wry smile.

"Feels better, doesn't it? The night, I mean."

He nodded. He did feel better.

"Come on."

"I can't," he said. "I have to go home. My friends are probably wondering about me."

He knew Charlie was going to give him an earful after running from Alexa the way he did but he couldn't explain it, the smell of her blood.

Jessica stepped closer. Her hand slipped around his upper arm and tightened.

"You can't," she said. "I'm sorry. You need to come with me now."

She tugged, pulling him forward a step before he braced himself and stopped.

"No," he said. "I'm going home." He pulled his arm out of her grasp and turned away. He felt better now. Maybe it was the night and maybe it was just him getting better but he'd had enough of the craziness. It was time to get back to his life. He would face Charlie's sarcasm and apologize to Alexa, if she still talked to him. The rest of this: sunlight sensitivity, enhanced senses or whatever, were just symptoms of stress no matter what some crazy woman said. He'd had enough of it and enough of her. He was taking his life back.

"Wait."

He heard her footsteps hurrying to catch up. He increased his pace but she managed to reach his side, keeping up as he crossed the street. A short cut between the photography building and the physics building would leave him just across the street from the lawn curving toward his dorm. Normally he didn't use the short cut at night. The lights overhanging the alley never worked or ended up broken. But he just wanted to get home.

His footsteps slowed as he approached the entrance to the alley. His shoes scraped on the sidewalk.

"Don't," said Jessica.

He whirled on her. "Leave me alone!"

He headed down the alley, his feet stomping. All his confusion and frustration had poured into that statement and now into his walk as he headed toward the other end. Enough, he'd had enough of weirdness. Enough headaches, enough smelling everyone and everything, enough hearing traffic miles away: enough, enough *enough*! He kicked at an empty beer can and listened to it scrap and tumble down the asphalt alley. Probably those physics guys, such partiers.

He didn't hear her footsteps and that was a relief. He didn't need some crazy woman spouting nonsense at him. Infection. Right. Maybe she was a friend of Charlie's and he was trying to teach Sebastian a lesson. That was something Charlie would do. A joke, taking this whole vampire nonsense and running with it.

Now it made sense.

He really had let it all get to him. He saw that now. He needed to relax. He was too high strung; he always had been. It had taken a mugging or dog attack or whatever to get him to realize it. He was overreacting and it had to stop now.

His shoulders loosened. He hadn't even realized how tight they'd been. If there was one thing that crazy woman was right about it was that he needed to eat something and when he got back to his dorm, he was going to hit the cafeteria and have the biggest steak he could fi...

Something slammed into his left side. He crashed to the ground. He felt a yank on his arm, flipping him onto his back. A figure rose up above him. A sour stench filled his nostrils. It was familiar; he'd smelled it before. Panic filled him. He yanked his left arm free and flailed at the figure. It growled, grabbing his wrist. He felt fingers closing on his flesh. Fingers! It was a person! It leaned over him, breathing out that sour stench into his face.

No, no, not again!

Racing footsteps approached. The figure reared up, away from him. Sebastian saw movement above him, something swinging. It smashed into the figure, driving it off him. The figure sprawled across the alley.

"Run!" Jessica screamed.

He scrambled to his feet. In the gloom he saw her standing with her legs apart, braced. She held something long in her hands. A baseball bat? A pipe? He couldn't tell. The figure on the alley shook its head and jerked around to face him. He caught an impression of long black hair, burning dark eyes, a mouth curled into a snarl.

A woman, he realized, his attacker was a woman.

She jumped to her feet.

"Run! Now!" Jessica commanded. She lifted the bat.

Sebastian turned and ran.

Even as his feet pounded on the asphalt, carrying him away, he thought he shouldn't be running, he should stay and help Jessica. But she'd told him to run, she'd said it. He reached the end of the alley and stopped. His heart pounded in his chest. He sucked in air through his mouth. From the alley, he heard a thump and a snarl then silence. He waited. His entire body tensed. Should he go back? Jessica might need help. He shouldn't have run, what kind of man was he to run and not stay to help? Shame filled him. He'd never realized what a coward he was. Maybe it was a good thing Alexa didn't want him.

He took a step toward the mouth of the alley, then another.

"Yes, come to me, little boy." The voice purred from the darkness. He wasn't sure if it was in the air or in his head. In that moment, he remembered the icy grip of her fingers and the stinging pain of her bite.

He spun and ran.

Part Two: Blood

CHAPTER SIX

Her laughter followed him all the way to his dorm, he could feel it in his head. In the elevator up to the fifth floor, he pressed his hands to his ears, trying to stop the sound before he realized it wasn't in his ears. It seemed to reverberate in his mind.

He really was going crazy.

By the time he reached his room, it had diminished into echoes, leaving his hands shaking as he opened the door. He stepped inside. Charlie sat on his bed, legs stretched out in front of him, a book on his lap. He snapped the book shut and swung his legs over the side as Sebastian entered.

"Where the hell have you been?" Charlie said. "I looked everywhere. Alexa was freaking out. She said you took off like a lunatic. Are you out of your mind?"

Sebastian felt hysterical laughter well up inside him as he staggered toward his bed. He landed heavy on the mattress. His hands clenched the sheets as he suppressed the laughter. No sense Charlie knowing exactly how crazy Sebastian was. His friend probably suspected but why confirm it?

"I was in the library." He managed to croak out the words.

"It didn't occur to you to call and tell us that?" Charlie said. "Sebastian, you look like shit."

Sebastian shook his head. He didn't understand what the hell was going on. Jessica, being jumped in the alley, the voice in his head, all of it whirled in his mind, finally settling on the one point he was sure of: the feeling of a bite on the side of his neck.

He jumped up. "I have to get something to eat." He stumbled toward the door.

Charlie stood and grabbed his arm. "Can you at least give Alexa a call? She's driving me nuts looking for you. She was about to call the cops."

"Okay, then food."

Charlie grabbed his cell phone from the desk and shoved it in Sebastian's hands. "Good, now call."

Much to his surprise, Sebastian's hands didn't shake as he dialled the number. The phone rang once in his ear before Alexa picked up.

"Hello?"

"Hi," he said.

"Sebastian, where are you? Are you okay? What happened?" Her words came out in a jumble as if trying to race out ahead of each other.

He rubbed a hand on his forehead. "I'm... I'm okay. I just had to get away. It's just been... I mean..." The words wouldn't come and he had no idea what he wanted to say. *I met a strange woman who seemed to believe I'd been bitten by a vampire and then when we left, a vampire jumped me?* It sounded crazy though he knew it was true.

"Okay." Her voice sounded more steady, more measured. He could imagine her sitting up straight, one slim hand resting in the lap as she held her cell phone up to her ear. She always cocked her head a little, as if holding the phone on her shoulder, even when she pressed it to her head with her hand. It was one of those quirky traits that he found so endearing.

"Do you want me to come over?" she said. "I could bring the notes from Friday."

He wanted her here right now, the comforting familiarity of her presence. She had this natural ability to make him feel better and lighter no matter what but as he pictured her he remembered the scent of her hair gel, her perfume, her skin, and then her blood and remembered how he'd thought how delicious she would taste.

"No, it's okay." The words rushed out. He took a breath. Steady, be steady. "I'm tired. I'm just gonna grab some dinner and go to bed."

"Okay." He thought he heard disappointment in her voice.

"I'll drop them off tomorrow then, okay?"

"That sounds good."

"How about around noon," she said. "We could grab some lunch."

"Yeah," he said. "I'm sorry I took off."

"It's okay," she said. "We'll talk tomorrow."

"Okay." He said his goodbyes and hung up, placing the phone back on the desk.

"Okay," Charlie said. "We're gonna get you some food and you're going to tell me what's really going on."

He crossed his arms and followed Sebastian down to the cafeteria.

Once inside, the actual prospect of food made Sebastian's stomach clench. He picked up a tray. He had to eat. Hadn't she told him that? Jessica. He remembered her leaning against the book shelf telling him he had to eat or it would overtake him.

The infection, she'd called it. Seeing that creature in the alley, he knew what it really was: vampirism.

He scooped some mashed potatoes onto a plate, piled some green beans beside and said yes to a pork chop.

"Take two," Charlie advised, following along at his shoulder. Sebastian nodded to two.

After getting his card punched, he followed Charlie to a seat beside the wall. At night, the floor to ceiling window at the far end acted almost like a mirror, reflecting back the occupants. Sebastian could see another him sitting in the window with the back of another Charlie across from him. He hoped that Sebastian was having an easier time of it than him.

He cut a slice of pork chop and scooped it into the mash potatoes before bringing it up to his mouth. He hesitated. Charlie's eyes narrowed as he spotted the motion.

"Eat it."

Sebastian stuck it in his mouth and chewed. Just like Jessica had told him, the food had no flavor. He chewed until it was mush and then swallowed. Maybe it just needed pepper and salt. He grabbed both from another table and added them. Cutting another bite, he chewed again. Still no flavor. He dumped more pepper on it. Charlie watched, his eyebrows drawing closer and closer together but he didn't speak.

One more piece. He looked at the piece of pork chop with mash potato and one green bean skewered on top. Black paper coated it in a thick layer. He would have to taste that now.

He popped it all in his mouth. For a moment, his tongue burned a little but then he realized he's scrapped his tooth across it.

No flavor. Nothing.

But his stomach had started churning.

He set the knife and fork down. A sip of water seemed to settle it a little. He sipped again.

"What are you doing?" Charlie said. "What is this weirdness with the salt and pepper? You never put salt on anything. I swear to god, Sebastian, you'd better start talking sense."

Sebastian set the glass down. "I met a woman in the library."

Charlie straightened from leaning halfway over the table. A slight smile curved his lips. "A women, eh? You finally decided to stop mooning over Alexa, huh?"

"I am not mooning."

"Right, and I'm a whiz at algebra. Tell me about the woman."

For a moment, Sebastian felt a flush of his old self, being indignant over Charlie's accusation although it was completely true but he could never tell Alexa that. Not after seeing her at the party Thursday, which of course brought up everything else. His moment of normalcy slipped away. He was left with the scents of everyone around him drifting through his awareness and the slight itch on his neck. And his stomach, it was gurgling again. He sipped more water.

Charlie spread his hands. "The woman?"

How much could he say, Sebastian wondered. Charlie would think he was crazy for sure, if he didn't already. But he couldn't keep this to himself. He needed help and there wasn't anyone else around.

"She said she knew what was going on with me," he said.

"Go on," Charlie said.

"The sunlight sensitivity, enhanced senses, all of it are because of ..." Sebastian hesitated. Charlie had dismissed this before, why would he listen now? His stomach tightened again. He took a breath to relax it. He had to try.

"Because of a vampire bite." He lowered his voice, leaning across the table toward Charlie.

Charlie's face was expressionless. "So some bimbo is buying in to your delusion, is that what you're telling me?"

Sebastian took in a deep breath. "You went out with Rod and Travis earlier. I can smell Travis's cigar on you."

Confusion twisted Charlie's expression. "What?"

"You ate something greasy then washed your hands with that industrial soap at the bar but you missed under your fingernails. Some of the grease is still there."

Charlie leaned back, staring at him. "What the hell?"

"I can smell it," Sebastian said. "Just like I can smell that girl's shampoo over there." He nodded his head at the brunette with the curls cascading to her shoulders. "It had papaya in it."

"Stop it," Charlie said. "You're freaking me out."

"Now you know how I feel."

"This is nuts. You can't expect me to believe you can smell this stuff because," Charlie leaned in and lowered his voice, "you got bit by a vampire."

Sebastian moved his fork around the mashed potatoes. "The sun hurts. It feels like it's burning my skin."

Charlie pulled his hands off the table. "Sebastian, you're just stressed out."

"That's what I thought," Sebastian said. "I thought it was just a reaction to everything but it isn't. It's true and I know it now."

"Why, because this woman said so?"

Sebastian nibbled on one of the green beans. His stomach churned at it and he soothed it with a sip of water. He put the glass back down on the table.

"It attacked me again on the way back here," he said. "Jessica fought it off. God, I should check on her."

He made to push the plate back but Charlie stopped it. "Sit down and finish," he said.

"But..."

"Ten minutes isn't going to make any difference now," Charlie said. "I want you to finish your food."

Sebastian sat down and picked up his fork. His stomach rebelled at the sight of the food but he knew he had to eat. A few bites wasn't going to stop whatever was happening to him. Somehow he knew Jessica was right, if he didn't eat a decent meal soon the change would keep accelerating and he would be lost.

He took another bite of the pork chop.

It was slow going. Each bite was small. He sipped water in between to settle his stomach. It felt like it took hours to finish one pork chop and a quarter of the potatoes but a glance at the wall clock in the cafeteria told him it was only fifteen minutes. His reflection in the bank of windows across from him seemed to be having just as difficult a time of it. Then he noticed a reflection of Alexa behind his reflected self.

He turned as she pulled out the chair on his right and sat down.

"How?"

"Charlie texted me," she said.

Across from him, Charlie waved his cell phone.

"What's going on with you, Sebastian?" Alexa said. "You have to tell me."

The scent of her filled his senses, almost making him giddy. He turned back to his meal, digging his fork into the second pork chop. Focus on the meat, smell that, not her.

"It's a little hard to explain," he said.

"Is this the vampire thing?" She leaned close whispering the words.

"You told her?" Sebastian said to Charlie.

Charlie shrugged. "What else was I suppose to do? You start talking crazy and then take off."

"I want to help," Alexa said. "Anything you need, Sebastian, I'll make sure you get it."

"I have to go back and check on Jessica," he said.

Alexa frowned. He could smell a sour distaste flowing off her skin. "Who's Jessica?"

"She's a woman Sebastian met who thinks he was bit by a vampire," Charlie said.

"Sebastian, she's just playing into a delusion," Alexa said.

"Well maybe," Charlie said.

Alexa tilted her head at him. "What do you mean?"

Charlie's hands fiddled with the cell phone in front of him. "Well maybe it is something. I don't know. I think we should talk to this girl."

"You don't actually believe this," Alexa said.

"You handled almonds sometime today," Sebastian said. "I can smell them on your fingers."

"What?" Alexa said.

"Will you stop that?" Charlie said. "It's freaking me out. He's been doing that all evening."

"How did you know that?" Alexa said. "I had some for a snack around two."

"I told you, I can smell them on your fingers."

She lifted her hand and sniffed at it. "I can't smell it." She rested her hand back on the table. She kept her expression carefully neutral but Sebastian didn't like the look of uncertainty in her eyes or the sharp tang of fear that drifted from her.

Great, now she was afraid of him.

He pushed the plate away.

"I can't eat any more," he said. "Can we just go?"

⌁

As much as Sebastian tried to talk her out of it, he was secretly pleased when Alexa refused to let them head out without her. Being practical, she insisted they take flashlights and weapons of some kind. Charlie had an old baseball bat in his room. The best Sebastian could come up with was an umbrella. He insisted Alexa take it.

For flashlights, they had a small one from camping and a mini LED one from Charlie's key ring. Sebastian was dubious as to its value until

Charlie turned it on, shining the bright white light on the sidewalk ahead of them.

"LEDs rule, man," Charlie said.

Sebastian had to agree.

He led them back toward the library, retracing the route he'd run less than a few hours before. He never should have left Jessica alone but her yell rang in his memory, almost a command that he had to obey. Strange, it had felt like that. His body had reacted without him really realizing it. A sense of unease grew in his mind. This just kept getting stranger and stranger. Was it all really happening or was he imagining connections where there were none?

He wasn't sure of anything anymore.

Except for the sour stench. He remembered that now. And the bite. His neck throbbed a little even as he thought of it.

"This alley here," he said. They stopped at the mouth of it because the red brick of the physics building. The dirty yellow brick of the photography building looked even duller and more faded in the light of the street light twenty feet down.

"I hear the physics guys do their drinking and carousing down here," Charlie said.

Alexa slapped him lightly on the arm. "Shut up." She hefted the umbrella and turned to Sebastian. "Let's go."

He switched on his flashlight and led them forward. As they edged deeper in the darkness of the alley, he realized he didn't need the light. His eyesight shifted and adjusted. Details he didn't notice in the day became obvious. The scrapes along the red brick. The streaks of dirt from the rain along the yellow brick. The asphalt lay littered with discarded cigarette butts. A few soda cans leaned up against the red brick. Unlike Charlie's joking assertion, Sebastian could smell only soda in those cans.

Halfway down the alley he caught a faint hint of the vampire's scent. He froze and inhaled deep into his lungs.

Here, she'd been here.

He shone the light on the asphalt. The layer of dirt here was disturbed, showing great swipes as if someone had been sweeping with large sweeps or someone had been swinging someone around.

Dammit, he shouldn't have run.

"I don't see anyone here," Charlie said. He flicked on his flashlight. The bright white of the LEDs flooded the area. Sebastian caught a glimpse of movement at the end of the alley.

"Hey!" he said.

The figure shifted to one side then began to move forward. Charlie swung the light at the figure.

"Turn that off!" A voice called. A woman's voice. Jessica, Sebastian realized. He headed toward her. Alexa and Charlie followed.

As he got closer, he saw she moved with an odd limping gate. She stopped about twenty feet from him.

"Who're they?" she said.

"These are my friends," Sebastian said. "Alexa and Charlie. Guys, this is Jessica."

"You're the one who fought the vampire," Charlie said.

Even in the gloom, Sebastian could see the raised eyebrow on Jessica's face.

"You should go back to your studies, little boy," she said. "There are scary things in the dark."

"Christ," Charlie said. "Sebastian, this is ridiculous. Let's get out of here."

"You should go," Jessica said. "You and the girl."

"The girl isn't going anywhere," Alexa said. "Until she knows what's going on."

"You shouldn't have brought friends into this," Jessica said. "It ends badly."

"I didn't bring them into anything," Sebastian said. "I came back to see if you were all right."

Jessica's head jerked back. "Oh, yes. I'm okay."

"The vampire didn't want your blood," Charlie said.

"She couldn't take my blood," Jessica said. "I'm poison to her."

"Huh?" Charlie said.

"I don't really want to stand here and discuss this," Jessica said. "It isn't safe here. I've got a place. Let's go there now."

"Not without us," Alexa said.

"Fine," Jessica said. "Not without you. Can we go now? Being out here in the open isn't a good idea. She's still looking for you."

"She?" Charlie said. "It was a 'she'?" He looked over at Sebastian. "You got taken down by a girl?"

"Shut up," Sebastian said. "Or I'm sending you home."

CHAPTER SEVEN

When she led them out of the alleyway, Sebastian saw the extent of Jessica's injuries. Fading bruises peeked out of the collar of her shirt. Her black vest looked even more faded with dust. She limped, holding her left leg stiff. The knuckles of her hands were torn.

"Are you okay?" Alexa said. She walked beside Sebastian, between him and Jessica.

"I'll recover," Jessica said. "Don't worry about it." She glanced at Sebastian but didn't say anything more.

They followed her off campus and down several small residential streets. Older houses squeezed together on small plots. Full grown trees spread their branches wide. They would form a natural covering over the street in the summer. Sebastian inhaled and smelled the differing buds blooming on the branches as well as the moist ground, hidden under the spoiled leaves from last fall. Even with the streetlights, the trees created a canopy from the stars, defusing the lights. Several trees stretched thick branches across the sky, as if trying to shield them.

From the houses, Sebastian heard sounds of regular life: TV, people talking, music, movement along wood floors or shuffling over carpet. He heard the sound of a child sighing as it slipped deeper into sleep. He caught the movement of Jessica's head as she glanced over at him. A slight smile curved her lips.

She heard all this too, he realized. Both Charlie and Alexa walked along, oblivious.

At the end of the street, Jessica turned right. Several small shops stood with darkened windows. It was too late for any of them to be open, Sebastian noticed, but Jessica walked up to the third one. A bookstore, he saw. Brammar's Books adorned the top.

"Back this way," Jessica said. She slipped down a narrow alley separating the bookstore from the convenience store on the corner.

Sebastian followed with Alexa right behind him. Charlie brought up the rear. Mud squished under Sebastian's shoes as he followed Jessica's limping form. He felt Alexa's hand grab the fabric of his sleeve.

"It's so dark," she said.

Sebastian clicked on his flashlight and pointed it on the ground at his feet. "Better?"

"Yes," Alexa said, the relief plain in her voice.

Strange, he hadn't noticed the darkness.

The end of the alley opened up into a small parking lot. A beige Toyota sat parked some distance from the door on the gravel covering the lot. Even with the gravel, Sebastian could see mud poking up from the ground. Drainage problem.

Jessica moved to the back door of the bookstore and tapped twice on the door. From inside, Sebastian heard a man's voice whisper, "Jessica?"

She glanced back at Sebastian as if to check that he'd heard. Of course, he'd heard the voice, it was clear enough. Then he realized that neither Alexa or Charlie had heard it. He looked away, glancing back across the darkened parking lot at the lone Toyota. Just another reminder of what was happening to him, of how strange he was becoming.

He didn't need another reminder.

He heard Jessica tap on the door three times. Then footsteps sounded before he heard the click of the lock and the hinges as they creaked while the door swung open.

"Who're these?" a man's voice asked.

"The In-Between and his friends," Jessica said.

"Why did you bring his friends?" he said.

"I didn't have any choice."

The man made a hrumphing sound then his footsteps retreated from the doorway. Sebastian felt Alexa tugging on his sleeve.

"Let's go," she said.

Of course he followed her inside.

The door closed behind him. He found himself in a darkened room. After a moment, his eyes adjusted and he could make the shapes of bookshelves lining the walls. Book cases stretched across every square surface, only the doorways broke the line. Even the back window on the left of the door was covered by book cases, he realized.

The musty scent of paper, glue, long dried ink, leather and cardboard hung in the air. A man, thin and short, stood beside the opposite doorway leading into the front of the shop. He reached behind the bookcase on the right. A switch clicked and the ceiling light blazed forth.

Both Charlie and Alexa stood blinking in the light. Sebastian blinked once and his eyes adjusted.

Jessica didn't even bother to blink.

Charlie swiped at his watering eyes. "So this is your place?"

"It's my place," the man said. His voice was deep and gruff. He didn't sound pleased to have everyone there.

"They all showed up," Jessica said. "I couldn't leave them out there. She's got his scent and she's still looking for him." She gestured to Sebastian.

"What's going on?" Alexa said. "Can someone explain that to me?"

"I still can't believe it's a 'she,'" Charlie said.

"Shut up," Sebastian said.

"All of you shut up," the man said. "Let me take a look at you and then we'll figure something out."

He crossed the room and peered in Sebastian's eyes. He reached up and cool fingers touched Sebastian's head. He turned Sebastian's head and peeled the collar back. Air brushed the side of his neck, on his wound. It made the wound tingle.

"How does it feel?" the man said.

"It tingles."

"Hmm." He released Sebastian's head and collar and stepped back.

"I'm Frank Brammar. This is my store as you've probably figured out. Jessica stays here when she's in town. I've got a room in the basement."

He paused a moment, putting his hands in his pockets. Sebastian heard his fingers scrape on something in his pocket. He tensed up. Was this Brammar going to try something?

Brammar's lips thinned. "You're right, Jessica, he's farther along than he should be." He pulled his hands from his pocket. They were empty.

"I know what happened to you and what you are now," he said. "You're an In-Between."

"Um, what's that?" Charlie said.

"It happens when a vampire doesn't get far enough in the feeding to either kill or turn the victim, but it's too far for them to ever be normal. You end up with some of the characteristics of a vampire, sensitivity to light, enhanced senses, preference for darkness, but as long as you don't feed on human blood, you won't fully change. You do have to remember to eat food though. Have you eaten?"

"I managed some tonight," Sebastian said.

Brammar nodded. "Good, that's good. For the first while, try to eat on a regular basis. It'll help. I know it probably makes you sick right now but you've got to do it. You're at a critical phase."

"This isn't really real," Alexa said. She glanced from Sebastian to Brammar and then back again. Sebastian noticed her rubbing her hand against the side of her pants, trying to wipe the scent of almonds from her skin.

"I wish it wasn't," Brammar said. "They took my sister years ago. She lived as an In-Between for twenty years until it got to be too much." A frown creased his face. "It won't be easy for you, not when you're so far along so fast."

"What do you mean got to be too much?" Sebastian said. "What happened?"

The man shook his head. "We aren't here to discuss that, we're here to discuss you. Jessica, were you able to identify the vampire who attacked him?"

"I caught a glimpse," Jessica said, "but she moved too fast. Long dark hair..." She shook her head. "Nothing else of any import."

"What about you?" Brammar said. "What do you remember of the attack?"

"Is there a reason for this?" Charlie said.

"If we know who the vampire is, we can maybe anticipate her moves. You're quite sure it was female?"

Sebastian nodded.

"Yes," Jessica confirmed.

"Okay, narrows things a little."

"Why?" Charlie said.

Brammar took a breath and huffed it out. "Are you always this irritating?"

"Yes, he is," Alexa said.

"Hey!" Charlie said.

Alexa bit her lip and started to giggle. When she looked over at Sebastian, he felt the tension surrounding his heart released. He felt his mouth twist into a grin and soon he was laughing too. After a few moments, it drained away but it had been a blessing while it lasted. He gave Alexa a grateful nod. She smiled.

"All done?" Brammar said. His voice sounded gruff but Sebastian noticed a trace of a smile on his face. The man noticed Sebastian's attention and the trace vanished. He pursed his lips and his eyebrows drew closer together.

"I really am curious about this narrowing down," Charlie said. "I'm not irritating." He threw a glare in Alexa's direction.

"Vampires tend to be organized in clans. Most clans are led by males but there are a few female led clans," Brammar said.

"Assuming it was a clan hunt," Jessica said.

Brammar frowned at her. "I'm trying to explain what we know for certain, not your conjecture."

Jessica folded her arms across her chest. Even without being able to sense it on her, Sebastian could tell she was irritated by the rebuff from the man.

"The best thing we can do is have you stay here," Brammar said. "I've got an extra room in the basement. I can monitor you and make sure you eat on a regular basis. You need at least another week to reach equilibrium."

"I can't stay here for a week," Sebastian said. "I've got classes."

"I'm sorry, you're going to have to forget about those for a while," Brammar said.

"Don't lie to him," Jessica said. "Tell him the truth."

"What truth?" Alexa said.

Brammar made to open his mouth but Jessica spoke up first.

"You can't go back to your life," she said to Sebastian. "Every moment in those classes you're going to smell every one of those people, every drop of blood in them. Even after you reach equilibrium, you'll still smell them and it'll always smell wonderful. The only people you can't smell are other In-Between. Vampires will just smell foul except for the one that attacked you, she'll always smell attractive to you."

Sebastian shifted in his spot. "What if I stay here for that week like you say, and reach that equilibrium? Will that help? Could I go back to class after?"

Brammar hesitated. He glanced over at Jessica. Her arms across her chest tightened.

Brammar's shoulders drooped. "No, I'm sorry. It wouldn't matter. It's like Jessica said. You can't go back. I'm sorry."

The words seemed to hang in the air in front of Sebastian, cutting off every image he'd ever had of his life: finishing school, maybe getting a Masters or getting a job right out of school. Sometimes in his dreams, he imagined Alexa with him, imagined their wedding, his working and them getting a little house somewhere. Commuting into the city, kids, weekends at home, picnics, throwing a baseball with his son or daughter, watching them grow, growing older with Alexa. All of those images, so clear and perfect to him, seemed to fade like an old photograph, ruined by sharp pain of a bite on his neck.

What would take their place? What kind of life would he have?

"No, that's not acceptable." Alexa shook her head. "You can't just say he can't go back to his life. Who the hell are you to say that?" Her voice rose, tinged with anger and hysteria.

"Yeah," Charlie said. His voice rose as well, his echoing fear. "You can't say that."

"I'm sorry," Brammar said. He held up his hands in supplication.

The bookcase covering the back window shattered. Books exploded into the room, hitting shelves and knocking other books to the floor. Several flew up to the ceiling, hitting the light fixture. It shattered, plunging the room into darkness.

Alexa screamed.

A figure leapt through the hole in the shattered window and twisted bookcase. It landed in a crouch, then stood up. Faint light from the hole filtered into the room. A sour smell filled Sebastian's nostrils. He realized it was a vampire smell and an underlying musk identified it as male.

It took two steps across the room and one hand shot out, grabbing Brammar around the neck. The vampire jerked Brammar off his feet and flung him back toward the door. Even before he landed, Sebastian could tell from the snap that echoed like a gunshot in his brain that the vampire had broken Brammar's neck.

Alexa sucked in a breath. Charlie made a soft noise in his throat. The vampire turned to face them. In the dark, Sebastian caught a glimpse of beard and dark hair swept back from a high forehead. Dark eyes seemed to glitter under his eyebrows.

"You would dare try to usurp me?" The vampire's voice rumbled low. Sebastian heard it in his mind as well and felt something pressing against his temples.

"No." Sebastian gasped the word out. It was hard to breathe. "I don't know you."

"She is mine," the vampire said. "I don't care what she promised you. I'll not stand for this. I made Bianca and she'll not make you."

The vampire took a step forward. His presence flowed over Sebastian in a wave of power. Sebastian's legs trembled. He felt his knees start to buckle. No, he couldn't fall over. Alexa, Charlie... This creature would kill them... He fought to stay conscious. Sweat trickled down his face, stung his eyes, and burned on his neck. The pressure on his lungs intensified. He opened his mouth, trying to suck in air.

Something flew past his peripheral vision. A book smashed into the vampire's head. It took a staggered step back. The pressure snapped away. Sebastian grabbed Alexa's arm.

"Run!" He dragged her toward the front of the store. He heard Charlie scrambling after them. Over that, he heard Jessica keep up a steady barrage of tossed books.

The front door was locked. He twisted the knob but it held. Dammit, he had to get them out of here! How long could Jessica hold the vampire off with books? His hand tightened on the door knob. He yanked as hard as he could.

The lock snapped. The door flew open. He staggered out, surprised. Alexa and Charlie fell out after him.

"Jessica!" he yelled back.

"Run!" Her voice called, followed by the steady sound of thumping books.

He shoved his flashlight into Alexa's hands.

"Run," he told her.

"But Sebastian..."

He shook his head. "I can't leave her in there alone. Not again. Go."

Charlie grabbed Alexa's arm. "Come on. Meet us at the dorm." He shoved the baseball bat at Sebastian. "Take this."

"Sebastian," Alexa said.

"Go." He turned away, unable to look at the pleading in her eyes. At first their footsteps staggered away then settled into a steady run.

He headed back into the bookstore wondering what the hell he was going to do in there.

He gripped Charlie's baseball bat tight and moved back toward the sound of steady banging books. He heard the vampire growl and felt a sense of impatience emanating from it. When it got too tired of this little game, it was going to snap Jessica's neck just like it had Brammar's.

Sebastian's heart hammered in his chest. His throat tightened. The bat shook in his hands. Swing with your body, he remembered his dad telling him over and over as he tried out for little league.

He'd sucked at little league.

He jumped through the door. Jessica stood crouched on the left, still grabbing books from the book shelves and whipping them at the vampire. It stood knocking the books away as if swatting flies. Sebastian swung the bat. He felt it slice through the air, picking up speed. He aimed for the vampire's face. One good hit...

A hand reached up and grabbed the bat, stopping it. It felt like Sebastian had slammed into a brick wall. The impact reverberated up his arms into this shoulders. Over the top of the bat, he saw the vampire smile.

"So glad you decided to come back," it said.

It yanked hard. The bat flew out of Sebastian's hands. The vampire tossed it back behind him. Of course he wouldn't need silly weapons like that, Sebastian thought. Already he could feel pressure start to build up around him, the effect of this vampire's attention.

"Bianca needs a little lesson about her place in the world," the vampire said. "Your death will be that lesson."

He took a step toward Sebastian.

Sebastian wanted to back away, tried to get his legs to move but the best he could manage was a trembling feeling in his knees. Another step and the vampire was that much closer. Pressure enveloped Sebastian, holding him in place, pressing against his lungs, his brain. The wound on his neck throbbed in time to his pounding heart. He could almost feel his blood racing through his veins. He imagined how it would feel soaking into his shirt when this vampire tore out his throat.

A shriek sounded from outside the window. The vampire spun around. Another figure leapt through the hole, flying across the space and crashing into the vampire. They fell into a heap on the floor at Sebastian's feet.

"Mine," a female's voice yelled. "He's mine, Constantine!"

The male snarled and backhanded the female astride him. She flew back, crashing into a bookcase across the room. Books cascaded down around her. She stood up growling.

A hand tightened on Sebastian's arm. "Come on!" Jessica's voice whispered in his ear.

She yanked, dragging him toward the front of the store. He stumbled after her. Every foot of distance from the vampires released the hold on him. By the time they reached the front door, he was running.

He sped out onto the street, then stopped when he realized Jessica wasn't with him. Where was she? He spotted her back at the door. She was kneeling on the doorstep, fiddling with something. He hurried back.

"Come on, let's get out of here!"

"They'll just follow our scent," she said. "We have to stop them." He saw wires in her hands. She twisted them together.

"What's that?" he said.

She finished, then jumped up and grabbed his arm. "Now let's go!"

She took off running, dragging him along.

They managed to cross the street and run several storefronts away before Sebastian felt an almost subliminal whomp. A hot wind slammed into his back, shoving him forward. Then the sound of the blast jolted the night. He glanced over his shoulder. Fire engulfed the bookstore. Flames shot out of the front window, spewing glass across the sidewalk. Smoke steamed from the roof, growing into steady billows in the night air. In the distance, he heard squealing car alarms responding to the sudden air pressure.

He felt Jessica's hand on his arm.

"Come on," she said. "We have to keep moving. If we're lucky that might slow them down for tonight."

"Slow them down?" he said. "That was an explosion."

"Yeah, slow them down."

Shit, he thought. Oh shit.

They ran as the first wail of sirens started in the distance.

CHAPTER EIGHT

As they ran, Sebastian realized Jessica was mumbling under her breath. He couldn't quite catch the words. Several blocks from the bookstore, he grabbed her arm, dragging her to a walk along the sidewalk.

"We have to keep going," she said.

"We are," he said, increasing the pace to a fast walk. "What are you saying?"

"We can grab a flight out tonight," she said. "I've got some friends in London we can crash with, then we should make our way east, maybe south east. Thailand might be good, we could hide there for a few years, stay off the grid."

"What are you talking about?" he said.

"We have to get out of here." For the first time he heard a hint of panic in her voice, stretching the tone into the higher range. "You don't understand who that is. This is a mess and we have to get out."

"Who is it?" he said.

She shook her head and he realized her whole body was shaking, possibly from shock as well as fear. He put a hand on her shoulder.

"Hey."

She shoved it off. "Look, I'm getting out of here. You want to stay and get torn to pieces in a vampire civil war, fine. I'm out of it."

She increased her pace, drawing ahead of him. It didn't take much before his longer legs matched her pace and he caught up her.

"Wait a minute," he said. "You can't just take off like this and leave me without any information."

"I tried to help you," she said. "If you'd come with me right away we could have prevented this. Frank might not be dead."

"I'm sorry about him," Sebastian said. "I didn't know. How could I? This is craziness, how was I supposed to react to you, to any of this? You say this happened to you too. Did you just accept it?"

Her thundering pace slowed. "No." Her head bowed. "I took it rather worse than you actually. Kind of drank myself into a stupor for six months. Would have been killed for sure if not for... some friends."

"Then can't you give me some time?"

She looked up at him. The dim street lights illuminated her frown. "I'm sorry, we don't have time."

"What about my friends?" he said. "I can't just leave them. My family, my school work."

"That's all over," she said. "The best thing you can do is walk away now before they get any more involved."

"Can you guarantee me if I run that these vampires won't go after Alexa and Charlie?"

She looked away from him, staring ahead along the sidewalk they walked.

"You can't, can you?" he said.

"It's still better," she said. "They might leave your friends alone."

"Or they might decide they want a midnight snack. Can you at least tell me how to fight them, if an explosion won't do it."

"An explosion would do it if they were still in the back when it went off," she said. "Their hearing and senses are even better then ours. They'd need less than a second to realize what was happening and jump out through the back door. Even if the fire caught them, they heal super fast. If we're lucky, it did hit them and they'll be out of it for the rest of the night. But they'll be back tomorrow night and even more pissed." She glanced back at him. "The best thing you could do for your friends is tell them to take a vacation for a while and for you to leave."

He frowned. "We're in the middle of the semester. That's not possible."

"Then I don't know what to tell you."

"We have to be able to fight them. There must be something, some way I can protect them."

She shook her head. "We don't have time for this."

He grabbed her arm and pulled her to a stop. "Then we make time."

She jerked her arm away, breaking his grip. "Forget it."

"Fine." He backed away from her. "Leave then. Save yourself. Why did you even bother talking to me in the library anyway? What was the point of that?"

Her lips thinned. A muscle along her jaw line jumped as she clenched her teeth.

He turned away from her and headed back down the street. "See you some time." Alexa and Charlie were back in his dorm room by now. Maybe they could find something on the Internet, some way to protect themselves until the vampires got bored.

Like that would happen.

Her footsteps scraped on the concrete sidewalk as she hurried to catch up.

"This is a damned stupid idea," she said.

But she followed him back to the dorm.

⁕

Sebastian couldn't believe it wasn't even past eleven when they reached the dorm. He felt like he'd been up all night but everything had happened in the space of a few hours. This explained why none of the floor monitors even blinked when he walked in with Jessica trialing after him. Curfew in their dorm wasn't until eleven. But even that was rarely enforced, although recently they had been cracking down a bit.

Sebastian led Jessica up to the fifth floor. When he reached his door, he had an absurd desire to knock, as if it wasn't has room anymore. He didn't like that idea and didn't want to examine it too closely. He grabbed the doorknob and turned.

Locked.

Now he did have to knock.

"Who is it?" Charlie's voice came out sharp and close by, as if he was standing just behind the door.

"It's me," Sebastian said. "Let us in."

"Who's us?"

"Me and Jessica. Come on!"

Through the steel of the door, he smelled the sourness of fear. Then the lock clicked back. The door swung open.

Charlie stood behind the door, holding an old golf club. He gave both Sebastian and Jessica a wary glance before he shut the door behind them.

Alexa sat on the desk chair, her feet pulled up onto the chair, her arms hugging her knees. As they walked in, she stretched her legs, setting her feet on the floor. Her eyes looked huge behind her glasses.

"You okay?" she said to Sebastian.

He nodded. "I'm okay."

She sat poised on the edge of her seat as if she was going to jump up and rush him but at his words, she relaxed. Her feet came back up on the seat and she wrapped her arms around her legs again, resting her chin on her knees.

"So." Charlie swung the golf club up and rested it on his shoulder. "Did you kill the vampire?"

Jessica frowned at him.

"No," Sebastian said. "But we blew up the bookstore."

"Really?" Charlie said. "Well, that's something then."

"You guys," Alexa said. She shook her head and then addressed herself to Jessica. "They won't stop, will they? They'll keep coming after Sebastian."

"Yes, that's right," Jessica said. She sat down on the edge of Sebastian's bed. Her shoulders sagged as she relaxed.

"Why?" Charlie said. "What's so special about him?" He jerked his chin at Sebastian.

Jessica took a breath and let it out slowly. "I tried to tell you, you're in the middle of a big power play. The vampire who tried to turn you wasn't authorized to do that."

"Authorized?" Charlie said. "She didn't fill out the right paperwork?"

Jessica stared at him and shook her head.

"Why did she do it if she wasn't supposed to?" Sebastian said.

Jessica shrugged. "Rebellion, trying to create her own clan, break out of that one. It could be any reason but the consequences are bad for you."

"Bad," Sebastian said. "Kind of an understatement."

"Define bad," Charlie said.

"The male won't stop looking for Sebastian," Jessica said. "He'll either want to kill him or turn him as a lesson to the female."

"Constantine," Sebastian said. "That's what she yelled."

"She who?" Charlie said.

"When I went back for Jessica," Sebastian said. "A female vampire came through the hole in the back yard, yelling at the male. They started fighting and that let us escape."

"And blow up the bookstore," Alexa said.

"She did that." Sebastian pointed at Jessica.

"I had to take the chance," Jessica said. "It might have worked."

"How do you know it didn't?" Charlie said. "Hey, maybe you blew them to kingdom come and we're worrying for nothing."

Jessica shook her head. "No."

"No? Why no?"

"We would have felt it," Jessica said. "It's unmistakable."

"What do you mean you'd feel it?" Charlie said. "Like some kind of psychic thing?"

"Yes," Jessica said.

Charlie looked like he wanted to say more but then he closed his mouth and shook his head.

"So how do we stop them?" Alexa said. "Do we hunt for them in the daylight and kill them? Where do we start looking?"

"This isn't a vampire movie," Jessica said. "They aren't just waiting in the basement of some castle, lying in their coffins, ready for you to stake them."

"So how do we stop them?" Sebastian said.

Jessica turned to him. He saw the fatigue and pain in the deepening lines around her eyes. Strange how it felt odd not to be able to smell it on her. How quickly he'd adapted to being able to use scents to figure things out about people. But she was still a blank to him. Was he just as blank to her?

"You don't," she said. "You don't have the capability. Constantine... he's too powerful."

Even without the scent of fear, the mention of Constantine caused a hitch in her voice.

"Constantine, that's the guy," Charlie said. "He's a bad ass?"

"The worst," Jessica said.

"So what can we do?"

"The best thing you can do is run," she said. "You and Alexa take off, finish your semesters somewhere else. At best he ignores you but at worst you're cannon fodder. He'll have your scents now and he'll realize what you are to Sebastian. He'll use them against you." She spoke that directly to Sebastian.

He swallowed. Was that true? Was his staying here endangering his friends? Charlie's knuckles blanched white where he gripped the golf club. Alexa's eyes were as large as saucers behind her glasses. The scent of fear almost dripped off them, filling the room. Did he have the right to subject them to what was happening to him? It was one thing to ask for support for his lunatic ramblings and the weirdness going on, quite another to expect them to risk their lives.

Maybe Jessica was right. Maybe he had to leave, at least for a while. Maybe after everything settled down he could come back. But what was he going to tell his parents? Could he even risk talking to them? He imagined they would nod understandingly all the way up to signing the committal papers.

"We aren't making any decisions tonight," Alexa said. She unfolded her legs from the chair and stood up. "There's got to be something we can do. You say he uses scents to track us. Maybe we can confound him somehow or use that against him. Maybe we can infect him with something, at least slow him down."

Jessica shook her head. "Nothing really affects him."

"Nothing?" Sebastian said.

"Well, they do have an allergy to garlic. It's an irritant but that isn't going to stop him for long."

"Are any of the vampire legends real?" Sebastian said. "Will any of that work?"

"Crosses don't do anything," Jessica said. "The only way to kill them is to pierce the heart and cut off the head, making sure it's pulled away from the body. I heard of one where the vampire's head was cut off but left there. The head reattached itself."

"Christ," Charlie said.

"Anything else?" Sebastian said.

"Fire, if you can get them to stand still for it. An explosion, but same thing. They're super fast and can sense things almost before you do them. We don't have the resources to fight here. The best thing to do is run."

"Don't have the resources," Sebastian said. "But you do fight them, with other resources?"

"Yes, but not here."

"Where then?" Alexa said.

Jessica sighed. "Elsewhere, with other In-Between. Ones who are stable."

"I'm not stable?" Sebastian said.

"Not yet," she said. "It'll take about a week for you to reach equilibrium. Until that time you're vulnerable to any vampire and Constantine can use that to turn you. After you reach equilibrium, he'll have to settle for killing you. You're poison to him after that."

"Poison? Why?"

"After you reach equilibrium only the vampire who started the process can finish it. Your blood is poison to every other vampire."

"That's why the female couldn't bite you," Sebastian said.

Jessica's lips thinned. "That's right."

Across the room, Charlie shook his head. He set the golf club down beside the door. "I've had enough of the weirdness for tonight. I could use a drink. Anyone else want one?"

"You're not going out," Sebastian said.

"Of course not, I'm going to Charlie's bar." Charlie walked over to the wall beside his bed. He rummaged in his locker and pulled out a bottle of whiskey.

"We have everything here at Charlie's," he said. "Rum, vodka, scotch, all in the form of whiskey."

He poured into Styrofoam cups and handed them around. Even Jessica took one and gulped the shot down before Charlie finished handing cups out.

"Whoa take it easy." Charlie splashed a little more in her cup. "We still have to make a toast."

"Oh? And what are we toasting?" Jessica arched an eyebrow.

"Surviving the night." Charlie raised his cup.

The disdainful look faded from Jessica's face. She lifted her cup to Charlie's.

"To surviving the night."

⤜∽⤛

They spent the night in the room. Sebastian found himself almost jumping at every creak in the building. With his newly enhanced hearing, he heard a lot of them. By two, most of the whiskey was gone. Charlie fell asleep on his bed. Alexa looked like she was going to topple over off the desk chair. Sebastian grabbed her shoulders and moved her to his bed. She curled up, her eyes closing as soon as her head hit the pillow. He listened to the deepening of her breath.

Here she was, in his bed. In all the months he'd imagined it, he never thought it would be like this. He sat down in the desk chair, facing the door. Jessica leaned by the doorway. Her arms crossed her chest, one hand still holding a Styrofoam cup. She drained the last of it.

"She's doesn't know, does she?" Jessica said.

"Know what?"

"How you feel."

Sebastian looked away. "That's not really your business." He stared at his hands, then noticed a drop of whiskey on his shirt.

Dammit.

"Sorry," Jessica said. "You're right."

He kept staring at his hands, at that stupid stain on his shirt. Even a half vampire or an In-Between or whatever, he still spilled all over himself. Good thing she hadn't been able to make him a vampire, he'd have spilled blood everywhere. Even the thought of it made him feel faint. He hated the sight of blood.

He would have made a lousy vampire.

He heard something hum. Across the room, Jessica pulled a phone from her back pocket. It vibrated in her hand but he heard it as if it was right up against his ear. She stared down at it and frowned.

"I have to make a call," she said. "I'll do it in the hallway."

Sebastian stood up as she unlocked the door and started to slip out. He grabbed her arm, stopping her in the doorway.

"Careful, we have hall monitors."

"Don't worry, they won't see me."

He released her arm and let the door click closed. It sounded as loud as a slam to him but Charlie and Alexa slept on. He turned to watch them in the gloom. Jessica had turned the light off when he put Alexa to bed. Shadows bathed the room in textures of grey and black. He had no trouble distinguishing anything. It was easier than during the day.

It was always going to be easier than during the day. That was just one way his life had changed.

He wasn't going to be able to stay here, he realized as he watched them sleep. He wouldn't be able to return to classes, not with his new sun sensitivity. He couldn't spend his nights locked up in this dorm room. Sooner or later, the vampire Constantine would find him. If not him, maybe the original one who'd attacked him.

Bianca.

He tried to remember her but all he had was a remembrance of the sour stench and a curtain of dark hair.

And the pain, yes, he remembered the pain.

His fingers touched the edges of the wound on his neck. Even after only a few days, it was already almost closed. Another few days and it might look like Jessica's, a scar on the side of his neck.

A constant reminder that he wasn't normal anymore.

He crossed to stand by Alexa sleeping in his bed. He held his hand out over her body, feeling the warmth radiating off her body. He could smell the sweet scent of her mingling with the scent of his laundered sheets and faint hint of his own musk. He closed his eyes. This was as close as he would ever get to her. It wasn't fair but he was coming to realize nothing was ever fair.

Frank Brammar probably would agree with that, if he'd lived.

He heard the light footstep outside the door before the doorknob turned. He opened his eyes and faced the door. Jessica poked her head in and waved him forward.

He took one final look at Alexa and crossed the room to Jessica. She held the door open, then let it close with a quiet click as he came into the hallway.

"I have to go," she said.

"What? You can't."

"I have to," she said. "I've got my orders."

"Orders?"

"This is a war, Sebastian. I can't wait for you to decide. Brammar had some important materials that we need. I have to get them before the cops."

"But what about Constantine?" he said. "The vampires are looking for us."

"I'm faster on my own," she said. "Look, I need a day or two to finish my business and then I'm out of here for good. I'll give you two days to decide if you're coming with me. We can help you adjust, give you a place and a purpose but you have to come then. You won't be able to change your mind. Once I'm gone in two days, I'm gone for good and you'll be on your own."

She took a step forward and put her hand on his arm. He felt the pressure of her skin but it felt so strange not to smell her, to get nothing but the scent of the dust on her clothes.

"It won't get easier," she said. "Neither one of those vampires will stop and you'll end up dead or turned. Neither is a good prospect."

She squeezed his arm and released it. "Two days. I'll meet you here Monday before dusk. You tell me what you decide then."

She turned and walked away before he could tell her that he'd already decided. He opened his mouth to call her back. But the words wouldn't come.

He listened to her footsteps echo away as she disappeared down the stairwell.

The wound on his neck tingled and he realized he envied her heading off into the night. His right foot slid forward an inch as if he would follow her then he turned back to the door and returned to watch over his friends.

CHAPTER NINE

Even with the sunglasses and hat pulled over his head, the sun gave him a splitting headache through the drapes in his room. He stood in the far corner, shoulders hunched, arms folded across his chest. He pressed his face against the wall, just barely turning his back to the rest of the room. On the bed before him, Charlie stirred. His eyes fluttered open. His mouth made a smacking sound.

"Are we vampires?" Charlie croaked.

"Not you," Sebastian said.

Charlie stretched, pulling his body to a mostly upright position. He glanced over at Sebastian's bed, then at Sebastian in the corner.

"Hmm?" Charlie cocked an eyebrow at Sebastian.

"She fell asleep just after you," Sebastian said.

"Where'd you sleep? Standing in the corner?"

"I didn't."

Charlie climbed out of bed. "You okay?"

"The sunlight."

"Oh yeah." Charlie pulled the drapes across the window, tucking them in at the sides. The room darkened, relieving the pounding in Sebastian's head.

"Better?" Charlie said.

"Yes."

Charlie crossed over to Alexa and shook her shoulder. She grumbled then shot upright, eyes wide. Her head darted from side to side.

"Where? Where?" she said.

"It's okay, you're in our room and not a vampire," Charlie said.

She took a deep breath and let it out. The pounding of her heart slowed. Sebastian could hear it from across the room.

"What time is it?" she said. "Why's it so dark?"

Charlie checked the alarm clock. "Just before ten. And the room is dark for our friend here." He waved at Sebastian in the corner.

"Sebastian, are you okay?"

"The sunlight, it's too bright for me," he said.

"Oh." She pulled her legs up to her chin and wrapped her arms around them.

Charlie stood by his bed, scratching at the mass of blond hair on his head. "I'm hitting the bathroom," he announced. "I'd invite you but the hall monitors might frown on it. They did with Bethany. Never understood that." He grabbed his bathrobe from the back of the door and headed out, mumbling under his breath about injustice.

The door clicked shut behind him. Sebastian crossed to sit in the desk chair beside his bed.

"Did you get any sleep?" Alexa said.

He shook his head. "I wanted to be awake in case..." He let the words drop away.

"Right," she said. "You should probably get some rest today. You got some catching up tomorrow."

"Alexa, I don't think I can go back to class," he said.

"Okay." She spoke the word slowly and deliberately. "You take a couple of days to reorient yourself. You can borrow my notes. Don't take too long though. We've got exams coming up."

"Alexa," he said.

She pushed the covers back and jumped out of the bed. "Goodness, I'm all wrinkled. My face must look a fright and my mouth feels gross. I have to head back to my dorm for a shower. Talk to you later, okay?"

She leaned over and brushed her lips against his cheek.

"Alexa..." He stood up but she was already through the door. It swung shut behind her. He made to follow. He got halfway down the hall when his feet slowed. What was he chasing her for? He had to leave. He knew it. He couldn't promise her anything else.

He returned to his room and sat on his bed. The space was still warm from her body. He took a deep breath, breathing in the last lingering scent of her skin. His cheek tingled where she'd kissed him.

If only...

Stop. He couldn't go down that road. 'If only' applied when you had a choice. He had none.

Charlie returned, body wrapped in the bathrobe, his clothes draped over one arm, his other hand rubbing a towel on his head.

"Where's Alexa?" he said.

"She went back to her place," Sebastian said. "She wanted to shower."

"Cool." Charlie dumped his clothes on the bed and towelled his hair with both hands. "Is she coming back for breakfast? We can talk strategy over waffles."

"I don't know," Sebastian said. "I don't think so."

Charlie pulled the towel from his head. His hair stuck up in every direction. On Sebastian, it would look messy and ridiculous. On Charlie, it looked tossled and chic.

"Hey," Charlie said. "What's up with you?"

"What's up with me?" Sebastian said. "Gee, I don't know. I was only bit by a vampire and now I can't stand the sun, can smell and hear everything, and that vampire wants to finish the job if the head vampire doesn't kill me first. I can't imagine what's up."

"Thanks for the recap, Mr. Sarcasm," Charlie said. "I get that. But I don't get this defeated tone from you."

Sebastian took a breath. "I have to go, Charlie. It isn't going to get better. The longer I stay here the more I put you and Alexa in danger.

Maybe the whole campus. I don't have the right to do that. I have to go. Jessica and her people can help me figure out how to live with this. You'll be safer with me gone."

"Oh," Charlie said. "You decided just like that."

"It wasn't just like that."

"Then what was it like? We don't get to talk about it? You just decide? What are you going to tell your parents, or are you not going to bother? Maybe just disappear, make them wonder for the rest of their lives what happened to you."

"Stop it," Sebastian said. "You think this is easy? You think I want to do this?"

"I think two days isn't long enough to make this kind of decision. I think maybe there's alternatives out there. I don't necessarily buy everything this Jessica says. How do we know we can't do something about the vampires? Maybe we can figure out a way to kill them and get it done. But running away isn't going to solve that."

Sebastian shook his head. "You don't understand."

"You're right, I don't." Charlie tossed the towel into the corner. "I'm going down for breakfast. You might want to take a nap, you look like shit."

He yanked on a t-shirt and a pair of jeans, shoving his feet into a pair of dirty running shoes. The door slammed behind him. He left the scent of his anger hanging in the air. It heightened Sebastian's headache.

Well, Charlie was right about one thing, he thought. He did need some sleep. He lay down on his bed and smelled the faint fragrance of Alexa on his pillow.

It took him some time to fall asleep.

The late afternoon sun didn't feel so bad after a good sleep, he realized as he lifted the drapes off the window. It only made his head ache a little. Was he adjusting to it, he wondered, or would it always give him a headache from now on. Maybe he needed to buy stock in pain relievers.

The room was empty. Charlie hadn't returned. Sebastian glanced at the clock as he got out of bed. Geez, after four! No wonder Charlie wasn't here. He'd probably been back and gone again but Sebastian had slept right through.

He grabbed a fast shower and changed into jeans and a burgundy t-shirt. A close inspection showed no food stains, not even after he put it on. A small miracle. Maybe he could build on that.

He let himself out of the room and headed for the cafeteria. He wasn't hungry at all but he knew he had to make himself eat, even though the thought of food made his stomach clench. Would you rather have blood? That thought made him feel dizzy. He grabbed the doorway to the cafeteria, fighting off a brief flare of nausea.

Steady, he thought. Food, get some food.

At the beginning of the cafeteria line, he grabbed one of the burnished steel trays. He pointed out a few items to the bored serving lady and ended up with half a tuna sandwich, a ladle full of macaroni and cheese, and a slice of apple pie that listed to one side. At the cash register, he added some juice and handed over his card to be punched. At least he had lots of room on his food card.

He picked up the tray and turned to the main room. Sunlight streamed through the large window, showing off the view of the courtyard out the back of the building. He squinted against the light. Damn, he'd forgotten his sunglasses upstairs. Too late to get them now.

As he stepped forward, a waving arm caught his attention. Charlie, sitting right by the window.

Of course.

Maybe he could sit with his back to the window. That might help.

He headed over, his eyes closed to slits. When he reached the table, he realized Alexa sat across from Charlie. She looked fresh and clean, her eyes bright and energized behind her glasses. She wore a soft butter-yellow, long-sleeved top and black jeans. He smelled the floral scent of her shampoo over his macaroni and cheese.

Sebastian set the tray down and motioned Charlie to move over.

"What?" his friend said.

"I want to sit with my back to the window," Sebastian said.

Charlie made a face. "Why, Miss Fussy?"

"The sun."

The smart alecky look faded. "Oh, sorry." He slid into the next chair over, leaving his old chair for Sebastian.

Although the smells of the food was enticing the first taste left him disappointed. The macaroni and cheese tasted flat. He motioned for the pepper. As Charlie handed it over, Alexa leaned forward.

"How are you feeling?" she said. "You look a little better."

"Getting some sleep was good," he said. He tried another bite. Even coated in pepper, it still tasted bland. He sighed. He was going to have to get used to it.

If his stomach would ever let him eat more than half a dozen bites.

"I've been looking on the Internet," Alexa said. "Dug up a lot of stuff about vampires, but nothing so far about the In-Between."

She pulled out an envelope of printouts.

"I've got some hacker friends trolling for the In-Between," Charlie said. "They should have something in a few hours."

Sebastian swallowed a bite of the tuna sandwich (bland) and sipped his juice (liquid bland). "Look guys, I really appreciate this but I don't think this is something that can be solved over the Internet."

"Who says?" Charlie said. "We've only begun to hack. I know a guy who knows a guy who did research with a guy who knows a guy from grad school that studied under a professor who claimed vampires were real and that he knew how to kill them."

Sebastian set his juice glass down. "I can't even follow that trail."

Charlie grinned. "Of course you can't, you're an idiot. Eat your lunch."

As he took another bite of the bland tuna sandwich, he caught Alexa smiling across the table. It almost felt normal, the way it always did. He and Charlie kibitzing with Alexa tossing in the occasional quip or smiling away. She was too polite to laugh out loud at him but her smile would grow to an almost breaking point. Charlie always said he wanted to get her to guffaw out loud but he hadn't managed it yet. He considered her refusal to laugh a direct challenge and Charlie loved challenges.

If it wasn't for the ache in his head or the way his neck itched or the warm, fragrant scent of Alexa's blood... He grabbed his juice glass and swallowed. Although it didn't have taste for him, the fragrance of the orange juice flooded his nose, drowning out the tantalizing small of her blood. Why had he fixated on her blood? Why wasn't Charlie's blood driving him crazy too?

Because you love her, you idiot.

He tried to push those words back into the recesses of his brain. He couldn't be thinking that now, not with her sitting right across from him. He felt like she could see right through him and if she looked at him, she'd know what he was thinking and that would be the final thing that would make her laugh.

He didn't think he could handle her laughing at him. Not now.

He tried a mouthful of the macaroni and cheese. Without flavor, it was like congealed goo in his mouth. Even as he tried to chew he could feel his stomach rumbling, daring him to swallow. Gonna toss it right back up, it seemed to be saying.

He chewed and chewed until it was mush in his mouth, but still he couldn't swallow it. He knew as soon as he did, his stomach would force it back up. Finally, he got up from the table, grabbed a bunch of napkins and returned. Holding two napkins to his mouth, he spat out the food and wrapped it up, then carried it to the garbage can. When he returned both Charlie and Alexa were staring at him.

"I couldn't eat it," he said. "It's just too bland."

"Do you want some ketchup?" Alexa started to rise.

Sebastian shook his head. "Don't bother. I can't taste anything anymore."

Alexa sat back down. "What do you mean?"

Sebastian explained about the lack of flavor. As he did so, he caught a whiff of that fear scent coming off her.

Not so much like the old days after all.

He poked at the remainder of the tuna sandwich.

"We're gonna figure something out," Charlie said. "We just need a little time. Right, Alexa?"

Across from them, Alexa nodded. "That's right. Don't give up hope, Sebastian."

He looked at their hopeful faces, nodded, determined, yet he knew they were lying. Their quickened heart beats and sour fear-tinged scents betrayed them. But how could he throw it back at them when they were trying so hard for him?

They were lying to him. He would just have to lie right back.

"You're right, guys. We'll think of something."

CHAPTER TEN

Sebastian heard the vibration before Charlie even jumped. Charlie dug into his pants pocket and pulled out his phone. He scanned the display then shoved it back into his pocket.

"If you're done eating, let's head out. We got places to get to."

Sebastian managed to finish the rest of the orange juice. He abandoned the remainder of the tuna sandwich and macaroni and cheese. He gave a wistful glance to the apple pie but couldn't bring himself to try it. He couldn't bear to have apple pie be bland.

Charlie poked him in the shoulder. "Come on, let's go."

He got up. Alexa stood waiting.

"Where are we going?" he said.

"Is this that guy?" Alexa said.

"The one and only," Charlie said. "Let's see if we can get there before sundown, okay? Sorry Sebastian."

Charlie hustled them out so fast he wouldn't even let them stop for Sebastian to pick up his sunglasses. Alexa offered him hers. They had big dark lenses and pastel pink frames. He hesitated as long as they were under the shade of some trees but as soon as they stepped into the full sunlight, he grabbed them and shoved them on his face.

Fashion be damned.

He certainly was.

His head still ached because he'd forgotten his hat. Thank god, Alexa didn't have a pastel pink number to match the glasses, he thought. He didn't think his dignity could bear that.

Charlie led them to the north end of the campus, down into the residential streets. Sebastian sighed with relief as they walked down a street shaded with large old growth trees. Older Victorian houses lined the streets, some with signs of renovation, the brickwork sand blasted or the lawns fully manicured. Others sat rundown, yellow brick coated with layers of dirt from the years, the lawns patchy and yellowed, not yet recovered from the winter. They reached a small one story bungalow set farther back from the street. The smell of cooked grease hung in the air around the place making Sebastian think that the occupant fried everything for eating, possibly even cereal. Charlie headed up the driveway, kicking stray pieces of gravel on the faded grey asphalt. Alexa followed while Sebastian straggled behind. He didn't want to get too close to her. The scent of her blood was too enticing.

Fortunately the greasy smell almost drowned it out.

Charlie bypassed the front door, continuing along the driveway toward the back. He stopped at the side door just before a faded wooden fence. The screen door creaked as he opened it, revealing a pale red wooden door. The paint was peeling from the top. The smell of grease was even stronger here.

Charlie knocked. Sebastian heard footsteps clomping forward on something that echoed a bit. Stairs, maybe? The door opened, revealing a tall, thin man with long, brown hair. Small granny glasses perched on his nose as he squinted at Charlie. He smiled, leaning his head back, revealing a high, balding forehead.

"Hey man, how's it going?" His voice drawled in a deep reverberation.

"It's going, Stan, going. These are a couple friends of mine, Alexa and Sebastian." Charlie gestured to them both.

Stan nodded. "Nice to meetcha." He stepped back from the door.

"Come on in. If you're here for the game, you're early. It doesn't start until three."

Charlie stepped forward, holding the screen door for Alexa. "No, we're not here for the game."

"Well, come on down."

Stan headed down stairs into the basement. Charlie and Alexa followed. As Sebastian closed the door behind him, he paused a moment, breathing through his mouth. The grease smell enveloped him and without the outside air, it was a little hard to take. After a moment, he adjusted and headed down the carpeted stairs. Could none of them smell the grease, he wondered. Had he been like them before? The stench of it was so obvious but when he reached the bottom of the stairs, none of them gave any indication of anything wrong.

The bottom opened into a large, sprawling living room. Green shag carpeting covered the floor. A sagging brown couch, the length of two regular couches, sat against the wall. Across the room, a fifty-inch flat screen television was bolted into the wall. In the center of the room, a large old wooden dining table sat covered with papers, game boards, dice and maps. Eight mismatched chairs sat tucked around the table.

"You guys want something to drink?" Stan said. "I've got soda, vodka..."

"We're good," Charlie said. "You texted me, remember?"

For a moment, Stan's watery hazel eyes remained vacant then he nodded, glancing over toward the small desk with a laptop sitting on it.

"Right, that's right," he said. "I did some digging like you asked. Weird stuff, man. Found some old forums buried deep, lots of security."

"Too much for you?" Charlie said.

Stan rolled his eyes. "Come on! No way, just took a little while but I got in. Searched for what you asked but I don't know what's in-between of. Sounds like some kind of weird cult thing, and they keep talking about vampires." He chuckled. "It's like they think they're real or something."

Charlie smiled thinly. "Right. Can I see what you got?"

"Yeah, sure." Instead of heading to the laptop, Stan crossed to the room to another door. He opened it and stepped through.

"Come in to the command center."

A large L-shaped desk sat on a raised platform. Three floor lamps stood shining down on the desk. A bank of monitors blocked the view until they walked around to the chair. An old, peeling leather chair sat in front of a keyboard. A large desktop computer sat on the floor by the chair. The hum of it and the monitors filled the room. Sebastian could almost feel the reverberation in his bones.

Various screen savers whirled or clicked on the bank of monitors. The geek hit parade, Sebastian thought noting Star Wars, Star Trek, and Lord of the Rings screen savers. Stan settled into the leather chair. A flick of a wireless mouse interrupted the screen saver in the center, a montage of the Munsters. Grandpa's face faded away as the image of a bulletin board appeared.

Neither of the vampires Sebastian had seen looked anything like Grandpa from the Munsters.

Stan scrolled through several screens. "Here we go. Let me pull it all up for you." He hit a button on a box half hidden by a candy bar wrapper. The other screens sprang to life, each showing a different aspect of the bulletin board. Different topics in the forum, Sebastian realized. He bent down to peer at one marked Italy. About half the topic titles looked to be in Italian, the other half in English.

"There's hundreds of posts here," he said, glancing across at the four monitors to his left. Another four sat on the other side of Stan.

"Thousands," Stan said. "Seems to be 'regional offices' so to speak." Stan used his hands to indicate the quotes. "Mostly they're location reports, supplies, stuff like that. The really interesting one is the main one. That's where they get into the whole vampire thing. I tell ya, it would make for a wicked RPG." He grinned and spun in the chair. It creaked under his weight.

"Yeah," Sebastian said. "Wicked."

Stan nodded as if Sebastian had agreed with him, not noticing the sarcasm. "I'd totally write it up if I didn't think these guys would come after me. The IP addresses are all over the world so I bet they got people over here and from what they talk about, I wouldn't want to mess with them."

"So the vampire stuff," Charlie said. "Do they talk about how to kill them?"

Stan turned back to the keyboard. The screens shifted again. The main forum expanded. With several clicks of his mouse, different messages scrolled across the various screens. He highlighted different portions on each.

"This is where it's cool," Stan said. "They report back on stuff that works and stuff that doesn't, as if they're actually trying it out." He snickered. "It's like they're making it up as they go. I guess they don't have a game master. Must be one of those crowd-sourced games."

"Must be," Charlie said.

"What do they have that works?" Sebastian said.

"Okay, I made a list." Stan's fingers flew across the keyboard. On the screen to his right, the forum display disappeared, replaced by a text page.

"This is what I got so far. Not much. Holy water, silver knives or bullets coated with pure silver. Sounds like anything made from silver or with a thick enough coating of pure silver, not just the silver plated crap. Cutting off the head is a biggie and so is staking them. Pretty typical, really. Garlic irritates them, slows them down but not for long. One of them tried daylight bulbs but it only irritates the vampires, doesn't kill them like sunlight. Cool, eh?"

"Anything else?" Sebastian said. "Any way to ward them off? What about inviting them in?"

"What's that?" Charlie said.

"That's from the movies," Alexa said. "You always had to invite the vampire in to your house first. Then they could come in any time after that."

Stan nodded. "Lady knows her vampire lore." He tipped a non-existent hat to her then he turned back to his screen. "Nope, that's not in there. Looks like their vampires can go anywhere but they don't want to be discovered. Something about not tipping the balance."

"What does that mean?" Sebastian said.

"Don't know. It's never defined. Lots of references to legends and stuff but they don't get specific. Nothing else to ward them off either. Just the silver weapons."

"There's got to be more," Charlie said.

"Sorry, dude. I'll keep an eye out but that's it. They talk a lot about where to find the best quality silver. Some of those pawn shops sell dirt cheap."

Sebastian took one look at the monitors and then turned away. He fished Alexa's sunglasses from his pocket.

"This is all really interesting but I have to go," he said.

"Sebastian," Alexa said. She started to follow him.

"Hey thanks, Stan. I'll get back to you." Charlie hurried after.

"Hey, you want me to keep monitoring?" Stan said.

"Sure!" Charlie yelled back.

Sebastian heard the door slam shut behind Charlie even though he was already all the way down the driveway heading back toward campus. Alexa's hurrying steps came from behind him.

"Wait up," she said. Her footsteps got louder, then he felt her hands grab his arm, dragging him to a stop. Her palms were warm against his skin. He would feel the warmth radiating from them, soaking into his flesh. The contours of her fingers almost touched his side. Through her skin, he could feel the hum of her blood as it flowed through her veins. It sang to him, inviting him, calling to him. Come, come for a drink...

He yanked his arm out of her grasp. "No!"

"What? Sebastian, what?" She looked startled. Her glasses reflected sunlight back at him.

He shook his head, trying to duck away from it. "I can't do this. I can't pretend anymore. I'm not going to get any better."

Charlie came jogging up. "Sebastian, that was just one guy looking. I've got others too and it wasn't a total bust. We found out about the silver."

"And the holy water," Alexa said.

"Enough, that's enough," Sebastian said. "You both saw that vampire last night. You think someone like that is going to be afraid of a little holy water and a silver letter opener."

"Not if you're holding them," Charlie said. "But some of us are a little more intimidating."

"This isn't a joke, Charlie." Sebastian yanked the collar of his t-shirt down, exposing his neck. "Does this look like a joke?"

Under the sunlight, the wound itched something fierce and he could only keep it exposed for a moment, then he pulled the collar back up. He could feel the sun pounding on his head. It didn't improve his mood any. This whole trip had been useless. Why did he have to come out in the daytime for such a useless thing? He rubbed at his temples.

"The sun is bothering you," Alexa said. She took a step forward. Her hand reached out toward him. "Let's get you inside some place, out of the sun."

He jerked away from her. "Don't. Don't touch me."

Her hand stopped in midair, then she pulled it back. Confusion and hurt crossed her face.

He could almost smell the pain coming off her. It distracted him from the call of her blood, helped him focus away from it. He shook his head, trying to clear it.

"I need to get back to my room," he said.

Charlie moved to his side. "Sure buddy, let's get you back." He put a hand on Sebastian's shoulder and turned him in the direction of the dorm. They headed that way with Alexa trailing behind.

All the way back, Sebastian could sense the hurt from her like the scent of a withering flower.

<div align="center">~~~~~</div>

When they reached the dorm room, Sebastian crawled into bed. The urge to pull the sheets over his head was almost overwhelming. He managed to just lay with his eyes closed, Alexa's sunglasses still resting on his face. For a few moments, he listened to Alexa and Charlie talking in quiet whispers in the hall. They sounded as if they could have been right by the bed, but he didn't pay attention to the words. Being out in the sunlight had drained his energy. He kept his eyes closed, allowing the buzz of the words wash over him. They faded into nothing as he fell asleep.

When he awoke after dusk, he felt a hundred times better. With the setting of the sun, his headache vanished. The darkness in the room seemed like midnight, even when he looked at the clock but then he realized Alexa's glasses still rested on his face. He took them off and the room sprang into focus, even in the dimness. It was so much more comfortable now without the glaring sunlight burning in his eyes, in his brain and on his skin. Darkness held the appeal of shadows, of depth, of texture. How could anyone not love it?

He climbed out of bed, feeling the sheets slide across his body. The room was filled with scents, Charlie's laundry in the corner, waiting to be washed, dust cooking in the laptop on the other side of Charlie's bed, the fading scent of laundry detergent from their clean clothes, and the mud on the bottom of his shoes, reminding him of walking among the trees. Had he even smelled the moistness of the earth that night or was he only able to smell it now?

It felt like that was his birth-place, or at least a place of passage into a new life. It really was a new life now; he was coming more and more to accept it. The soothing darkness, the rich smells around him, everything made him feel more alive. He didn't have to be just a gawky, pathetic college student. He could be something else. He was In-Between.

He could maybe be even more.

If he was really going to leave maybe he should visit his birth-place, his place of passage one last time. From Stan's monitors he knew most of the In-Between were in Europe so he wouldn't be back here in the New World for a long time. Maybe he'd never come back to school, so why not say goodbye to that spot where his life had changed?

He shoved his feet into his running shoes and made sure he had his wallet. His hands skimmed the desk, finding what he needed. There, that was everything. He'd visit briefly then return to pack up his stuff.

He moved through the dorm, catching echoes of other students, circling around and away to avoid them. He didn't want to see anyone now, not even Charlie or Alexa. Alexa... The thought of her brought a twinge of anguish, almost breaking through the dream-like quality he was feeling in the night. He wanted to say goodbye to her before he left, wanted to tell her how he felt but was that fair? Was it fair to say it and then leave? But if she didn't care it wouldn't matter. Of course she didn't care, a little voice said inside him. If she did, wouldn't she have said something by now? She was braver than he was, of course she would have spoken up. She would probably nod sympathetically and be secretly glad he was leaving because then he wouldn't be pestering her anymore.

Best to leave talking to her until after he'd visited his birth-place.

Outside the dorm, the air smelled sweet and fresh, with a hint of exhaust from the cars along the main street to the north of the campus. He breathed deep, tasting the tang of budding leaves, rich earth, dust, and the infinite variety of people. How amazing they all smelled. The differences in skin and hair, of sweat and breath.

Of blood.

Two girls walked past him as he crossed the lawn. One redhead, one blond. The redhead caught his eye as he inhaled, drinking in their scents. He stared at her, unwavering in his attention. She faltered, falling behind her friend, slowing almost to a stop as she looked back at Sebastian. Her mouth opened a little bit. A vacant look came across her face. He could hear the beat of her heart slowing and under that a deeper throbbing, almost subliminal in its depth.

The beat of her blood pulsing through her veins.

His mouth watered.

Her head drooped to one side. A tiny bit of dribble gathered in the corner of her mouth.

"Stacy?" He heard the other girl speak.

What the hell was he doing? He yanked his gaze away and stumbled off, not paying attention to the direction, just anywhere else than these two girls. He heard them speaking to each other, their voices following him as he hurried off.

"I don't know," he heard the redhead say. "I just don't know."

Her voice echoed like an accusation in his head. But an accusation of what? He didn't even know what he was doing, if he was actually doing anything. He was just going for a walk, he just happened to look at a girl. Was there anything wrong with that?

There was now. There was something very wrong now. Because that wasn't just a look and this wasn't just a walk.

His feet carried him on and he soon found himself crunching through a carpet of old leaves. They squished and crackled under his feet, releasing the smell of old decay and moist earth. He even smelled the pungent scent of earthworms, coming up through the ground to feed on the leaves. Everything returned to the ground, he thought.

"Not quite everything."

The voice spoke from over his right shoulder, a deep, sultry voice.

He caught a whiff of a familiar sour smell. He'd never heard her speak before, just that single scream of a name. *Constantine.*

He turned.

She stood leaning against a tree, her arms crossed over her chest. It didn't seem a particularly vampiric pose to him, no arm crossed over her lower face, leaving only her hypnotic eyes. When she smiled, the corners of her eyes crinkled just like a regular person. Dark brown hair curled around her face and down to her shoulders. She wore jeans and a darker shirt. He wasn't sure but he thought her fingernails were painted pink.

"It's Hollywood pink," she said, spreading her left hand in front of him, displaying the nails. "That's what it said on the bottle. They give them such silly names."

"You're..."

"Bianca." She smiled again and bowed her head. "You've been quite a challenge for me to catch up to again. I didn't realize it would take this long."

"Didn't realize what would take this long?" he said.

"Our bond. I thought it would happen instantaneously even though Constantine always had to wait a few days. I always thought that was a sign of weakness. Imagine my surprise to find out it's just the way of things." She chuckled, a deep throaty sound that made him dizzy. He wanted to take a step back but his feet wouldn't move.

"Why me?" he blurted out.

Her head tilted. "Why you? I've been watching you for some time. You have the natural look for a vampire, tall, dark hair, pale skin. You don't stand out in a crowd, you'll be able to infiltrate perfectly. At this age, you can wander any campus around the world and always look like you belong there." She stopped. "Do you believe any of that? You were alone and walked by. Why not you?"

"That was it?" he said. "You changed my entire life on a whim?"

She pushed away from the tree, her arms swinging free as she took a step toward him. "What other reason is there? Would any other reason make you feel better? Maybe if I declared undying love? Ha, undying!" She laughed at her own joke.

He felt despair settle on him. No reason, just a stupid mistake. He'd walked through the trees at the wrong time. If he hadn't stormed out of the party, if he'd stayed and talked to Alexa, so many ifs and he couldn't change any of them, couldn't take anything back. The despair flared into anger. He clenched his fists.

Her smile widened. "Oh yes, there's the temper. It makes you smell so sweet, almost as sweet as that night." She inhaled deeply. "Ah, you smelled so delicious then. It's almost as good now." She took another step forward. "It wouldn't take so much to finish it, just another taste. It's horrible to be caught in this limbo. I'm sorry I left you there. I didn't intend it but they came on me too fast. I had to hide, then Constantine..." She stopped and shook her head.

"Don't you worry about him. He's a weak fool. I can make you strong. You'll never have to worry about the burning sun again."

The sour smell of her filled his nostrils. He should be disgusted, repulsed, and indeed those emotions did seem to be there but they were distant from him, locked away in a part of his mind that wasn't important. Don't pay attention to that. It doesn't matter. All that matters is the smell of her in front of him, the way her mouth smiles, exposing the sharpness of her teeth, the touch of her hand on his arm, encouraging him to tilt his head just so, revealing the wound on his neck, the healed membrane so thin, covering the entrance to a new life, a better, everlasting life. The stench of her enveloped him as her head moved closer. Her mouth opened wider.

His left hand dug into his pocket, grabbed the object inside it, pulled it out and jabbed at her. The iron scent of blood overpowered her stench. Her scream filled his ears, breaking the spell. He stumbled back as her hands came up to her cheek where he'd scratched her with the silver grapefruit spoon.

Beneath her hand, her cheek festered and bled. Her lips pulled back, no longer in a seductive smile but in a fierce snarl. Gone was any trace of normal humanity, she carried the rage of a monster.

"Mine!" she snarled.

He stumbled back several steps. She advanced until he held up the silver spoon. The blood on the jagged tip looked like it was smoking.

"Stay back," he said. "I'm not yours."

Her face twitched. She straightened from her crouch, moving in an awkward, disjointed way, as if having to force herself to stand up. Impassivity fell like a mask over her face although he could see her rage smouldering in her eyes. Her hand still pressed against her cheek. It wasn't festering quite so much now.

"You don't really want to do this," she said. "Stay like this. You'll never fit in anywhere with any of them. As much as you want it, you're not human anymore. You're more like me than them. You've smelled their blood and wanted it, I know you have. Maybe just once or twice, but it will grow. It will drive you mad if you don't drink. If you drink without turning more, you'll make yourself sick. You'll wish you were dying but you won't. And once you start that way, even I can't help you."

The edges of the spoon handle bit into Sebastian's palm as he gripped it. Was she right? He knew he couldn't stay here, couldn't be around Charlie and especially around Alexa. Hell, he couldn't even allow himself to be around regular people, if he could gauge from his reaction to the girl passing him on the lawn. If she'd been alone, if he'd felt the hunger more keenly... He couldn't even let himself finish the thought.

But what about Jessica and the other In-Between? Would they accept him? She'd seemed surprised at how quickly the changes had overtaken him. Was it that much different for him? Would it cause problems?

Maybe the only choice was to complete the change. If Bianca had not been interrupted Thursday night, he would already be turned. He wouldn't have had to endure these few days of torment. He would be revelling in his new power, his new life at her side...

He shook his head then stared at Bianca. She was staring fixedly back at him. She was doing this, planting these thoughts in his head. He stumbled back several steps. When she moved forward, he held up the spoon. She stopped.

"I won't," he said.

"You're a fool," she said. "I can set you free."

"Condemn me you mean," he said. "What about Constantine? He didn't seem too thrilled that you were branching out on your own."

She scowled. Touched a nerve, he thought.

"You have to finish turning me," he said. "You'll lose face if you don't, maybe lose more. Will he cast you out? How well does a vampire like you survive on her own?"

"Well enough," Bianca said. "He'd never cast me out. I'm his favorite."

"Favorite, right," Sebastian said. "If you're so favored, why did you go against him? He doesn't seem too pleased that you're trying to change me."

She dismissed the notion with a wave of her hand. "Constantine is old fashioned. He believes the clan leader is the only one who can do the changing. But this is a new century, we have to change with the times. We need new members who can navigate this new world. You would be such an asset to us, Sebastian. You have a place with us. You'll never feel ignored or awkward. None of the females will turn you away. You belong with us. We will be your family. And if it's still so important to you, we can bring along a few others."

She'd moved within a few inches of him. He could smell the sourness of her breath beneath the promise of her words. *Bring along a few others.* He knew exactly who he would choose to bring. He could give her eternal life, then she'd never turn away from him, she'd always be grateful, always be willing...

Alexa...

He started as Bianca's fingers stroked his cheek. What? No! He jumped back, swinging with the spoon. He didn't even come close to Bianca but she scowled and dodged away, breaking her spell on him.

He had to get away from her. Somehow she was getting into his head, twisting his desires. He didn't want to do that to Alexa, he didn't. The words howled in his mind.

"Who do you lie to now?" Bianca said. "You and I are connected. I know your soul, little boy. You are naked before me. Shall I show you everything you want? All the nasty, dirty, evil things?"

"Shut up!" He stumbled back. She advanced, staying just out of reach of the silver spoon.

"You know I'm speaking the truth. You feel it. It's all right to feel those things, to want those things. You can have them, I can help you have them. I can help you have her. As many times as you want, the ways you want."

"Stop it!" He had to shut her up, he couldn't keep listening. Desire and disgust rose up inside him, but he had to push them down, had to think. She wanted him overcome by his emotions, confused and upset, then she could pounce. He had to fight back, had to control himself.

But she knew exactly what to say, knew his darkest fantasies, ones he could barely bring himself to admit. Their connection, he realized, when she started to turn him they had connected and if she could read him so easily, maybe he could turn it on her.

Okay, focus, Constantine. She wanted to usurp Constantine. Why? The image of a young boy rose in his mind. Thin, clothes of rags, dirty face but smiling, laughing, skipping down the street, racing ahead and then coming back, tugging on her hand, calling out, *come on, momma, come on, the circus!*

Julian.

Then the shadow in the night, darker than any darkness, a bite full of pain and sweetness. Life slipping away, draining into hunger, raging, overwhelming hunger. So hungry, starving, doubling over with the pain of it. A hollowness in the stomach, in the soul. Wailing hunger. Demanding hunger. Must be FED!

And the boy sleeping, facing the door, skin so warm, so pink. He wakes up, eyes blinking away sleep.

Momma?

"I won't be Julian for you," Sebastian said.

She stopped moving. Her mouth opened in shock. "How can you?" Her face tightened in anger. "You can't do that!"

"Looks like I can," he said. "You drank your own son. Did Constantine make you do that or did you just decide to do it yourself? I couldn't really tell just then."

She shrieked and lunged forward. He swung with the spoon, scratching her across the face. She howled as the silver raked her skin. Her hands came up. She stumbled to her knees.

Before she could get up, Sebastian ran.

He ran for his life.

CHAPTER ELEVEN

When he broke through the trees, his feet automatically veered toward his dorm, toward home, toward safety. He took ten steps before he stopped himself. It wasn't safe, not for him, not for his friends.

He couldn't go back there. Not with Bianca trailing him. She'd know how to find him. He was like a flashing sign to her. Would he ever be able to outrun her?

He had to find a way, had to think of something. He forced himself to slow down to a walk and turn away from the dorm. He couldn't involve them anymore. No matter how much Charlie and Alexa wanted to help, he couldn't let them, couldn't risk them. His chest hurt at the thought of Alexa. He'd wanted to... he imagined... He couldn't let those thoughts back in. Part of him wanted to pretend Bianca had implanted the ideas, forced them into his mind but he knew the truth, knew there was a dark place inside himself that welcomed the idea, and wanted to drag Alexa down too because then he could possess her.

He'd never have to feel the pain of wanting again.

But he couldn't do that, wouldn't do that. It was an illusion. He wanted her love, the way he loved her but that wouldn't be love. If he did that, if he allowed himself to be changed all the way, he wouldn't even feel love anymore.

There wasn't much choice left, he realized. He had to find Jessica. She had to help him. Maybe she'd even know a way to break this bond with Bianca. At least then, he'd be free of that.

How could he find her? He didn't even know her last name. He couldn't even smell her. Even out in the middle of the campus he knew if he concentrated he'd be able to find Charlie or Alexa. Their scents stood out to him against all the others. But Jessica was blank. He'd never find her that way.

How had she even found him in the library? Think. There had to be a way for him to track her down. If it wasn't by smell, it had to be something else. In the library, she'd known already, known he'd been bitten but not fully turned. How had she known? If he was In-Between like her, she couldn't smell him either but she'd known.

Dammit, think!

Was it the same way as with Bianca, some kind of psychic thing? He'd never believed in that stuff but a few days ago he'd never believed in vampires.

Funny how life could change so fast.

His thoughts kept whirling in his head. He had to find a place to relax, some place safe that Bianca couldn't follow him. A dry chuckle caught in his throat. Where the hell could that be?

In the end, he headed for the small chapel on the outskirts of the campus. It had a bland seventies look to it, plain pews, simple marble altar. Simple silver twin bowls containing holy water sat on either side of the main aisle. He hesitated in front of the bowls. Could he touch it? Would it burn?

He didn't want to find out.

He didn't want to feel more cursed than he already felt.

Soft lighting illuminated the interior of the chapel. He was alone although someone had been in here recently. He could smell their lingering scent. A woman, he could tell from the floral perfume. He chose a back pew, moving toward the end, as far away from the scent as possible.

The wood of the pew felt hard beneath him and against his back. He rested his hands on the wood beside him. Funny, they didn't burn. Maybe he wasn't so cursed.

Yeah, keep telling yourself that.

So, how was he supposed to do this? He'd had this idea but he had no idea of how to try it. At least with Bianca he'd felt it, had her presence and her own reading of him to guide him. He didn't have that with Jessica. Maybe he should just think of her. He pictured her in his mind, the first time he'd seen her in the library, leaning against the bookcase. Brown hair pulled back in a ponytail that trailed over her shoulder when she tilted her head to look at him. A full head shorter than him but with a strength in her, the curve of her arms and shoulders, her smooth, easy movements, twisting to pull off her backpack, arching her back, her breasts pushing against her vest.

He closed his eyes, remembering how she'd jumped to his defence immediately, not once but twice, first against Bianca and then against Constantine. Even after Frank's death, when she must have been grieving, she'd helped him. She was even going to come back Monday to see what he'd decided.

After checking on Brammar's materials.

His eyes popped open.

Brammar's home. That was the place to start looking.

He left the chapel, pulling out his cell phone to start searching for Brammar's home address. Something in him felt certain Jessica was there.

He only hoped Bianca couldn't read him well enough to beat him to it.

<hr>

Brammar had lived in the west end of the city. Sebastian flagged a cab down and sat huddled in the back seat, staring out the window. Even through the glass barrier, he could smell the driver, a mix of body odor and cologne. But under that, he could smell the man's blood, a rich, invigorating smell that seemed to hover in front of his nostrils. He stared out the window, trying to focus on the passing buildings, the streets, the trees, the parking lots, anything but the blood.

He gripped the silver spoon tight in his left hand until it dug into his palm.

Anything, anything for the distraction.

When they finally reached Brammar's house, Sebastian tossed several twenties at the driver and clambered out of the seat, not waiting for change.

"Thanks buddy!" the driver called but Sebastian hurried away down the sidewalk. He sucked in the scents of the lawns, the dust on the street, the pollen in the air, all to drown out the smell of the tempting blood.

The cab drove away. Sebastian faced the small red brick bungalow. Brammar's house. He headed up the walk.

A quick glance around showed no one watching. He tried the front door but it was locked. Even without the neighbors looking, he didn't want to break in through the front. He hurried around the back, letting himself into the small backyard through a chain link fence. He crossed a small patio of cobble-stone. A barbeque sat to the right of a patio door. Two folding patio chairs leaned against the wall.

Sebastian stared at the barbeque. It was such a regular thing. He could imagine Brammar out here in the summer, making burgers, enjoying the sun, adding cheese and bacon to his burgers. Juice would probably drip from his chin as he ate the burgers. He'd have to wear sunglasses against the brightness but he'd still lift his face to it and enjoy it.

"Actually he won't anymore."

He hadn't noticed the sound of the patio door sliding back. Jessica stood in the doorway, hand still on the door handle. Her expression was as blank as her scent.

"What are you doing here?" she said.

He swallowed. His mouth felt dry. "How do you do that?" he said.

"Just answer my question," she said. "I don't have time to play teacher."

"Bianca," he said.

Something flickered across her face, then her mask of impassivity locked down. "So?"

"I can't stay here," he said. "I get that now. Bianca can read me. She wants to get back at Constantine for turning her."

Jessica frowned. "How do you know that? Did she tell you?"

He shook his head. "She didn't have to."

Her eyes widened. "You can read her?"

"Um, yes. Couldn't you read the one who bit you?"

"No," she said. "None of us can read vampires, only other In-Between." She pushed the door open farther. "Come in."

He stepped into Brammar's house. She slid the door closed and drew the drapes. Then she turned on a light. Ordinary living room furniture filled the room. A couch sat against the wall with two arm chairs on either side. An old console television sat opposite.

"Sebastian, there's something different about you," Jessica said. "You aren't developing the way a normal In-Between does."

"How do normal In-Between develop?" he said.

"Slower for one thing. The sun sensitivity doesn't start to kick in for a few days. The blood lust another day or so later. By then we've had time to prepare them. Given them some tools to help combat it."

"There's a way to stop it?"

"No, you can't stop it," she said. "But it's controllable." She frowned at him. "For most of us it is."

"Tell me," he said. "I need to control it and I need to find a way to keep Bianca out of my head."

"I don't know how to do that," Jessica said. "As for the blood lust, it's a mix of meditation and relaxation techniques. Things we don't have time for right now. Once we're out of here, I'll start training you. For now, you just have to avoid people as much as possible."

He spread his hands. "That's it? That's all you can tell me? Meditation and relaxation will help take away this craving? Are you serious?"

"Sebastian, I'm telling you what works for us. It does work but it takes time and practice. We don't have the chance for either right now. You're going to have to be patient."

"Patient! I don't think Bianca's going to be patient. I think she's going to do everything she can to turn me as soon as possible." He took a step toward her. "Please, I need help. I'm... I'm afraid I won't say no next time."

There. He'd said it aloud to her. His shoulders hunched. He felt his stomach pull in as if waiting for a blow. Was she going to call him a freak? Maybe she'd pull out a stake and stab him with it. Kill him now before he could be turned.

Maybe that wouldn't be such a bad thing.

Instead, her shoulders sagged. Her eyebrows crinkled together and her frown loosened into an expression of sadness.

"I'm sorry," she said. "I'm so sorry."

Her misery startled him. Before he could react, she took a breath and shook it off. The same business-like expression settled on her face.

"We can't get out of here until Monday night, early Tuesday morning at the latest. That leaves us the rest of tonight and tomorrow night to avoid Bianca, and by extension, Constantine. You can be damn sure he's still looking for you. He doesn't have the same link with you as Bianca so it'll take him a little more time, but he's got your scent now from Frank's bookstore." Jessica gestured around the room. "I still need a little more time here and then we can go. I know of a safe house we can hide in. The vampires will have a hard time finding us there."

"Hard time? How?"

"Let me finish here and I'll explain on the way. Okay?"

"Okay," he said.

She nodded and headed deeper into the house. He stood in the living room, wondering if he should follow her. The patio door leading to the backyard made him nervous. He remembered how easily the vampires had smashed through the window at the bookstore, as if it were tissue paper. He didn't imagine this patio door would pose that much more of a barrier to them.

He headed into the hallway. Without the ability to smell Jessica, he had to stop and listen for her. He was almost annoyed at not being able to smell her. He'd adapted so fast to this new life.

He didn't like that very much.

He heard the scrape of furniture from downstairs. He turned right down the hallway, trailing his hand along the wall until he came to an open door. Even in the darkness, he could see stairs leading down. He headed down them.

The basement opened into a warren of rooms. A small TV room sat right at the bottom with an open door leading off to the right. He moved through the doorway and found himself in an office. Jessica stood at a pair of filing cabinets. Her head jerked up as he entered.

"What is it?" she said.

"I didn't want to wait up there," he said. "Can I wait here?"

Her head turned a little toward the filing cabinets then swivelled back to him. "No, not in here. Wait in the family room." She nodded her head to indicate the small TV room.

"Oh, okay."

He retreated back into the small TV room. He felt chastised, like a kid who'd bugged a parent while they were working. He listened to the scraping of the cabinets and the shuffling of paper. She wouldn't let him help, he could tell that without even asking. She didn't trust him and why should she? She'd already told him he wasn't developing the way other In-Between did. Maybe it was already too late, maybe he was turning but slowly. Maybe Bianca had been more successful that she realized.

"Don't be ridiculous."

Jessica appeared in the doorway. She finished stuffing several sheets of paper into her backpack and zipped it up. She swung the pack over her shoulder, arching her back to hook it onto her other shoulder.

Sebastian stood up from the couch he'd sat on. "What?"

"You're just being paranoid," she said. "You aren't turning slowly. It doesn't work that way."

"How can you be so sure?" he said. "It's happening faster than with any others. Maybe I am turning."

She shook her head. "No, you aren't."

"How do you know?"

She sighed. "If you were, you wouldn't be able to handle the sun at all. And besides..."

"Besides?"

She stepped closer to him. He smelled the musky scent of paper coming from her back pack.

"You wouldn't have been able to stay in a room with your two friends and not drink them."

Sebastian felt all the tension clenching his shoulders upward drain down through his body, leaving him feeling rubbery. The thought of that... He couldn't articulate it. It was too upsetting.

In front of him, Jessica nodded. "See? You aren't turning. If you were, you wouldn't care who they were. All you'd want is the blood. Understand now?"

He nodded, not trusting his voice.

For a moment, a crack of compassion broke through her mask. She put a hand on his shoulder and squeezed.

"Come on. Let's get out of here. You need to rest. It's been a hell of a night for you."

He stuttered a harsh laugh. "Yeah."

She smiled and released his shoulder, turning toward the stairwell. As she lifted her foot to step up on the first step, Sebastian grabbed her arm, stopping her. His head tilted up, listening. She turned her head.

"Wha...?"

His hand clamped on her mouth. He shook his head. Her eyes widened over his hand. Her head gave a nod. He released her. Her mouth stayed firmly shut. Her gaze jerked upward, then back to him. She could almost see the question in the expression on her face.

What is it?

He'd heard... something. He wasn't even sure what it was, not a step, not a door sliding or a fabric rustling but something. He knew they weren't alone here. He could feel it.

He could feel it in the sudden sourness, the sudden cold that seemed to waft down the stairs.

Bianca.

Somehow she'd tracked him down.

He tapped the wound on the side of his neck and pointed upward. Jessica's mouth thinned. She pointed back toward the small office. They crossed the carpeting and tiptoed across the thin linoleum of the office floor. Another door led into a workshop. Pale moonlight filtered in through a small window near the ceiling.

Jessica tapped him on the arm and pointed at the window. He nodded.

They crossed to the workbench under the window. Sebastian expected her to climb up on the bench and open the window, but first she poked through the tools, pulling out long screwdrivers with narrow tips. He tugged on her sleeve and pointed at the window. She nodded and made several hold on gestures. He shook his head and tiptoed back to the door.

The feeling of Bianca close by increased. It would be only a minute or two before she zeroed in on him for sure. What the hell was Jessica waiting for? He turned back to her. She waved him back. He hurried over to her. She shoved several screwdrivers into his hand.

He mouthed "what?" at her.

She mouthed something but he couldn't tell what she meant. She tried once more but when he still didn't get it, she shook her head and started climbing up on the workbench. He climbed up after her.

She tugged at the lock but it wouldn't move. He could tell from the look of it that it was probably rusted shut. He put his hand over hers. Together they focused on twisting the lock open. It held fast, resisting, then he felt a minute shift. He nudged Jessica. One more try. They twisted again. With a grind that seemed to echo through the house, the lock scraped across, opening.

The window started to fall open. Jessica grabbed one side, Sebastian the other. They let the window down easy but it still creaked.

It sounded so loud he thought it drowned out the pounding of his heart. He felt sweat trickle down his back. If Bianca caught him in this room...

He had nowhere to run.

He felt Jessica's hand on his arm. She jerked her head up. Him first.

He shook his head no and pointed at her.

She gave one nod and reached up for the window sill. Even standing on her toes, she couldn't get enough leverage to haul herself up. He interlaced his hands and bolstered her up. The backpack just cleared the top of the window by an inch as she slithered through. Her upper body vanished, then her torso and legs, then finally her running shoes. After a moment, her form blocked the moonlight again and he could make out her face. She waved him forward and held out her hand.

He reached up to the window sill. It was easier for him to get a proper grip since he was so much taller. Still he took her hand, appreciating the warm feeling of her skin as she pulled. He poked his head out, then his right shoulder.

Jessica's hand jerked out of his.

He saw her fly backwards, sailing through the air to land flat on her back. She rolled onto her side, groaning.

A leg stomped in front of his face, blocking his view. He looked up. Bianca.

"Who's that little bitch?" she said. "I don't like you seeing other women."

He tried to duck back in but she grabbed his hand and yanked. He felt his body scrape against the edges of the window as she dragged him out.

The cool wetness of the grass felt good against his cheek when she dumped him on the ground.

"I don't like you running from me." Her voice growled as she crouched by his head. "Why are you fighting me so? You know you'll give in, you know you want to."

He felt her hand on his head, stroking his hair. She let her hand run down his shoulder and his back, cupping his buttocks before returning to his head again.

"Why don't you stop pretending when you and I know what you want."

The sour sweetness of her breath filled his nostrils. Her voice hummed in his ear, in his head, travelling deeper down, loosening his resistance, his resolve. He didn't really have to do anything really, just stop saying no, just tilt his head a little. Just a bit. He wouldn't even feel a thing...

Her scream jolted him. She fell over and he saw Jessica standing there, hands braced on her legs. She reached down with her left hand and slapped his cheek.

"Come on, snap out of it!"

He staggered to his feet. Bianca rolled on the ground, her arms struggling to grab at the screwdriver plunged into her back between her shoulder blades. She shrieked again. Her back arched impossibly, her hands flailing.

Jessica grabbed his arm and pulled.

"Come on, before she gets that thing out of her back. She'll heal up fast once it's out."

They started running down the street. Jessica soon fell behind, limping. He slowed to help her.

"Where are we going?" he said.

"Cab, find us a cab," she said.

He glanced up and down the street. "I think there's a bar on the next block. We can find cabs there."

Sure enough as they got close, he was able to flag one down. Jessica climbed into the back. As he followed, and the cab moved away, he thought he saw a familiar curtain of black hair move in the shadows between two houses.

"She's following," he said to Jessica, keeping his voice down.

She glanced out the back window but the cab had already taken a right turn. "Are you sure?"

He nodded.

She frowned. After a moment, she shrugged off the backpack and rifled through the contents. Then she leaned toward the driver.

"Change of plans," she said. "When's your shift over?"

The man glanced at her through the rear view mirror. "Huh?"

"We want a tour of the city. Start in the west end and just keep driving. Stay in the populated areas."

"Ah, lady."

She held up a fistful of bills. "I have enough."

"Yes, ma'm." He turned his attention back to the front.

"What about the safe house?" Sebastian said.

"We can't go there with *her* following us." Jessica faced the back window as she whispered in his ear.

"We can't lead her to populated areas," he said.

"It's safest," she said. "Bianca may get distracted, might find it harder to track you with others around. If we can lose her there, we can head to the safe house."

"And what if she feeds on someone, because she's following me?"

Jessica pulled her head back so she could face him. "What makes you think she wouldn't anyway?"

~ ✦ ~

They had to drive around for almost two hours before Jessica thought it was safe enough to leave the cab. Sebastian climbed out and stared around at the neighborhood of suburban houses while she settled the bill.

As the cab drove off, she started walking. He hurried to catch up.

"How much did that cost?" he said.

"Don't worry about it," she said. "I talked him down."

Something about her tone made him look at her closer. "What do you mean?"

A brief smile crossed her face then vanished. "You'll learn. Let's get indoors. There's still an hour or two before dawn and I want to be inside."

She just kept shaking her head when he tried to press her so he gave it up and followed. All the houses had the same generic look to them. Cookie cutter houses, he'd always thought. Even the drapes in all the front windows looked the same.

Jessica turned up the walkway to number 67. She pulled out a key and unlocked the door. As she opened it, she put her finger to her lips to signal him to be quiet. He nodded and followed her into the house. She closed the door behind him then entered a code into the alarm system by the door. She grabbed his hand and led him forward.

To his surprise, the house looked furnished. He could see dark shapes loaming in the living room and dining room. He wanted to ask her about it but remembered her motioning him to be quiet. She opened a door and started to move down. Stairs. He followed, closing the door behind him.

At the bottom of the stairs, she opened another door. He walked into a room of complete blackness. Even his new night vision had trouble making anything out. He heard the click of the door closing, then a flare of light as she flicked on an overhead light. The room contained a cot along the wall with a table and two chairs against the other wall. A small fridge and sink with built-in cupboards above sat opposite the door. A small door by the foot of the cot sat closed but he imagined it led to a bathroom.

"What is this?" he said.

"A safe room," she said. She waved at the beige walls. He noticed flecks in the paint.

"Silver flakes," she said. "Repels vampires."

"Why silver?" he said.

"We think it's a severe allergy but we're not sure. Same with holy water."

"Do people live here?" he said. "Are we putting anyone in danger?"

"Sometimes people are here, upstairs," she said. "Not right now though."

Twisting her shoulders, she pulled off the backpack and set it on the table. Then she drew out one of the chairs and sat down. She gestured at the cot.

"You take that. You could use the rest after tonight. I'll need you sharp tomorrow night so get as much rest as you can."

"But..."

"I'm serious. The more well rested you are, the easier it is to resist the cravings or Bianca's influence."

"Okay," he said. He sat down on the side of the cot. Even sitting made him aware of the weariness inside him. He felt like he hadn't slept in days. Already his eyelids drooped. He bent over to untie his shoes. He felt his cell phone digging into his thigh. He dug it out of his pants pocket and set it on the bed beside him. Surprising it still had a signal down here. He wondered if he should call Charlie and let him know he was all right.

The phone rang just as he finished the thought.

Great minds think alike, he thought as he picked up the phone. But it wasn't Charlie's number.

"Who is it?" Jessica said.

He frowned. Why would Alexa be calling him at this hour?

He hit the answer button and brought the phone up to his ear. "Hello?"

"Hello, Sebastian, isn't it?" A deep male voice purred in his ear. "You and I should have a chat, boy. We have much to discuss."

Sebastian felt as if his chest had caved in. He hunched over.

Jessica jumped up from the chair and rushed over.

"What? Who is it?"

Sebastian managed one word.

"Constantine."

CHAPTER TWELVE

"Are you still there, boy? You need to listen."

"I'm here." Sebastian croaked the words out. Jessica sat beside him and squeezed close, trying to listen as well.

"As you may have surmised, I have your lovely friend here. Very pretty. You have good taste, boy. I will agree to a trade. You for her. Come tomorrow night."

"Come where?" Sebastian said.

Constantine's voice chuckled on the phone. "Oh, I'm not going to tell you right now and have you rush over early. That would be rude of you. I'll call you tomorrow night and set up the location and time. Leave that other In-Between behind. If there's any sign of her, your friend here will die or worse."

"How can I be sure you won't hurt her anyway?"

"You can't, boy, but you don't have any choice," Constantine said. "And just so you think I didn't just steal her cell phone..."

Over the phone, Sebastian heard a rustling, then a frantic breath came on the line.

"Sebastian! Don't come, please..." Alexa's voice, pleading.

"Alexa, I'm sorry I…"

"No!" Her voice wailed then cut off.

"That's enough," Constantine said. "She's still alive as you heard. She'll stay that way until you come tomorrow night. Come alone and I'll let her go. There's just one other thing."

Sebastian tried to swallow in a dry throat. "What?"

"Make sure you bring Bianca as well. Both of you come, or no deal."

The phone clicked off.

He kept holding it up to his ear, as if it would come on and everything would be different. A joke. Maybe Charlie and Alexa were playing a sick joke on him after everything he'd put them through the past few days. He wouldn't blame them. A joke, it had to be.

Please let it be a joke.

But he knew it wasn't.

"No!" He whipped the phone at the wall. It hit above the table, smashing into pieces and spraying to the floor.

The effort had brought him to his feet but he sank back onto the cot, putting his head in his hands. He felt an arm around his shoulders, then Jessica's voice in his ear.

"I'm sorry, Sebastian, I'm so sorry."

Her voice sounded warm, soft, comforting but it wasn't the right voice. It wasn't *her* voice and it would never be her voice. He could almost accept that if he'd known she would be safe, if he knew Alexa would have a regular, normal, happy life. He could live with that, live with not being a part of it. But now, she'd never get that and it was his fault.

He tried to hold it in but it was too much, everything was too much and he ended up sobbing into his hands.

Jessica's arm never left his shoulder.

~✦~

He pulled himself together after a few minutes. When he started sniffling, Jessica handed him some tissues to blow his nose. She got up from the cot and moved to her backpack, giving him a moment to sort himself out.

He wiped his face, removing any trace of tears, and he felt his own mask clamp down. It felt like it slammed over his entire body, his entire soul, leaving him numb. He'd never feel anything again.

He waded up the tissue and tossed it at the bin beside the fridge.

"I'm going," he said.

Jessica turned around. "I'll go with you."

He shook his head. "He won't let you come."

"That's later, when he gets in touch with you again." The toe of her running shoe poked at one of the pieces of his shattered phone. "He'll have to find another way."

Dammit, he hadn't thought... He closed his eyes. He'd ruined Alexa's one chance. He'd as good as killed her.

"It's okay," Jessica said. "You can call Alexa's number and leave a new number for him to call you at."

"Good idea." He headed past her toward the door.

"Where are you going?" she said.

"Back to my room," he said. He hoped she didn't ask why.

She didn't ask.

The sun was just starting to rise when he came out of the house. Of course, he didn't have his sunglasses. The rising sun sent shooting pain through his head but he didn't care. He wanted it. It was a better, cleaner pain than the one that ate at his heart.

Jessica followed, hurrying to catch up. She shoved a hat on his head. The brim shaded his eyes a little, lessening the pain. He tried to yank it off, but she held it fast to his head.

"Stop it," she said.

He acquiesced.

It took them a little over an hour to get back to the campus. Sebastian was surprised it only took that long but then again they weren't wandering the streets, trying to stay near crowds and avoid a vampire.

"We have to find Bianca," Sebastian said halfway home.

"Don't worry about that," Jessica said. "She'll find you."

By the time they reached his dorm, the pain throbbed steadily in his head. His shoulders hunched as his head bowed down. Jessica steered him inside and then toward the stairwell. In the cool dimness, his headache lessened. She tugged on his arm and he climbed, turning when she indicated and stopping when she stopped.

He moved to open his door and began to twist the knob when it was yanked out of his hand. The door flew open. Charlie stood in the doorway, blond hair dishevelled. He grabbed Sebastian by the shirt and dragged him inside. Jessica hurried forward before the door closed.

Charlie hurled him across the room. Sebastian landed sideways sprawled over his bed.

"Where the hell have you been?" Charlie yelled. "I thought you went all..." He made vague gestures with his hands.

"No," Sebastian said. "I didn't." He pushed himself up to a sitting position.

Charlie took a breath and pushed his hair back from his face. "Okay, okay. Just don't leave for the whole night without saying anything, okay? Leave a note or something."

He turned away, digging through a pile of clothing at the foot of his bed, mumbling something about "drink" and "shower."

"We've got a problem," Jessica said.

Charlie pulled out a towel and a robe. "We'll discuss when I get back."

"He's got Alexa," Sebastian said.

Charlie froze halfway to the door. He turned in slow motion.

"What?"

"Constantine. He's got Alexa."

Charlie stared at Sebastian then turned his gaze to Jessica. She nodded.

"He wants Sebastian to come tonight, with Bianca. Them for Alexa," she said.

"Fuck," Charlie said.

"We've got today to plan," Jessica said. "We don't know where the meet will take place but I can make some assumptions."

"What do you mean?" Sebastian said. He stood up and took a step toward her. "You can't come. He'll kill her if you show up."

"Relax," she said. "I'll stay far enough away but we can still plan strategy. Just because he's offering to trade doesn't mean we want to let him take you, Sebastian."

"She's right," Charlie said. "Can we get Alexa back too?"

"We're going to try."

Sebastian shook his head. "I'm not playing with her life. I won't do it."

"You can't just let Constantine call all the shots," Jessica said. "You have to plan for contingencies."

"She's right," Charlie said.

Sebastian shook his head. He couldn't do it, he couldn't risk Alexa that way. Couldn't they see that?

Jessica grabbed his arms and shook him, forcing him to focus on her. "Listen to me, Sebastian, Constantine wants you. You're what he wants and that's leverage. You don't have to be passive in this. You can make demands of your own."

"He'll kill her."

"Not right off. Keeping her alive will bring you to him and he knows it. As long as your demands aren't too overt, we might be able to influence where the meet up will be. Maybe we can turn that to an advantage."

"How?" Charlie said.

"I have to think." She released Sebastian's arms and sat down on the foot of his bed. The backpack made her look like a hunchback.

Charlie hovered halfway between the door and the bed. Finally he shuffled toward the door. "I'll be right back." He slipped out as if escaping.

Sebastian sat down beside Jessica.

"Will he really do something that I ask?" he said.

"Maybe," she said. "If you ask properly and if we can think of a place he won't object to. Some place small with multiple exits."

"Why multiple?"

"It'll be harder for him to cover all of them, especially if you've got Bianca with you."

"What about the old planetarium dome on the other side of campus?" Sebastian said. "It's got multiple exits. They're boarded up but we could break through some of them."

She nodded. "That's a good idea. You should get some rest. I'll pick up some supplies and be back." She checked her watch. "By eleven and we can head over there."

"I'll come with you," he said.

"No, you need to rest."

"What about you?"

"I've been an In-Between longer, I don't need as much rest. I can go for days without it if I have to, you're still adjusting."

"I can't just sit here."

She put a hand on his shoulder. "I need you to rest so you're ready for tonight. She needs you to be sharp tonight. Get it?"

He nodded. She stood up and crossed to the window, peering out around the corner of the drapes. He saw sunlight poking through and it made him wince. She pulled sunglasses from her vest pocket and slipped them on her face.

"I'll be back by eleven," she said. "Make sure you rest even if you can't sleep."

"Okay."

She left and he didn't even hear her steps in the hallway. She moved in silence.

Charlie returned a minute later, a towel wrapped haphazardly around his head. He landed on his bed with a thump and sat staring at the floor. The towel tipped and fell off, leaving his hair a dripping mass.

"It's my fault." Charlie's voice sounded muffled under his hair.

"What?" Sebastian said.

"It's my fault." Charlie looked up. "I left her alone."

"Charlie..."

"If I hadn't left her alone..."

"It's not..."

"He never woulda got her."

"...your fault."

"It is!"

"It isn't." Sebastian crossed to sit beside him. "If you hadn't left her alone, he would have got both of you."

Charlie didn't say anything. He sat with his head bowed, hair dripping onto the towel on the floor. Then his voice came in a low mumble, "Wouldn'ta got me."

Sebastian shoved him in the arm. Charlie half fell but caught himself. He flipped his hair back from his face.

"I'm coming with you."

"No, you aren't," Sebastian said. He stood up to cross back to his bed. Charlie's hand shot out and grabbed his arm, fingers tightened around his forearm.

"Yes, I am."

The steel tone in his voice made Sebastian glance over at him. The goofy, laidback, fun-loving Charlie was gone, replaced by a serious faced young man. Even with a mass of wet, unruly hair dripping water down his face, his expression demanded consideration. Alexa was his friend too, Sebastian knew. Maybe there was some way he could do something without being in too much danger.

"Okay," he said. "But you stay back with Jessica. I don't want you too close. They can use you against me too."

"Okay." Charlie nodded and released his arm. "So what's the plan?"

Sebastian sat back down on his bed. "We're thinking the old planetarium."

Charlie's nod became more enthusiastic. "That's a good idea. There's catwalks around the dome interior, places to hide."

"You won't be hiding there," Sebastian said.

Charlie waved off his objections. "We'll argue about that later. How are you going to get Bianca to come?"

Sebastian frowned. "That's a good question. I don't think she'll come voluntarily. She claims she's Constantine's favorite but I think he's pissed at her."

"For what, trying to turn you?"

"Yes, I don't think she's allowed to do that."

"Probably you won't be loyal to him," Charlie said. "Can only be one queen bee in the vampire hive."

"Something like that, I suppose."

"There might be something there," Charlie said. "Maybe we can pit them against each other."

"And we slip out during the fight," Sebastian said. "If it's only that easy."

"Might be worth a try."

"We'll have to get Bianca first."

"No, first we have to eat breakfast. And that means you too."

"I'm supposed to wait here for Jessica and rest."

"Eat first and then rest." Charlie stood up, grabbing some clothing. "You're supposed to eat food, remember."

Sebastian sighed. "I remember."

He managed a piece of dry toast and several bites of scrambled eggs. Even with ketchup and pepper, they had no flavor. The coffee was a little better. Some of the bitterness of the straight, black coffee came through. Before he'd hated bitter but having something with a bit of flavor was better than the bland, cardboard taste. How would he ever get used to this?

Charlie had a class at nine thirty. Sebastian insisted he attend and come back after. Charlie protested but Sebastian pushed him out the door, saying he needed to rest and couldn't if Charlie was hanging around.

"You won't leave without me," Charlie said. "Promise. I want in on this. She's my friend too."

"I promise," Sebastian said.

He almost even meant it.

He listened to Charlie's footsteps echo down the hall as he walked away. He didn't want his friend involved, it was just one other person to worry about. It would be hard enough to stay focused with Alexa in trouble. When Jessica got back, he'd make sure she kept Charlie back.

And what about Bianca? How as he going to get her to come along? She certainly wasn't going to come willingly, not if Constantine was angry with her.

He lay down on his bed and put his arms behind his head, staring up at the stucco ceiling. Flakes of paint curled around the joins where the walls met the ceiling. Sloppy work.

Maybe he should pretend to let Bianca finish the job with him. Then when she got close enough... what? Tie her up? He didn't think any rope would be strong enough to bind her. Handcuffs? She might even be able to break those too.

Would he even be able to resist her? He remembered the hypnotic spell she cast on his thoughts. Could he even trust himself around her? He had to, it was the only way to save Alexa.

He'd been such an idiot with her, he saw that now. He should have said something to her, tried at least, but he'd been too afraid of rejection. Too afraid she'd turn her back on him completely and he'd lose all of her. At least if he never asked, he still had their friendship.

And what of that now? Because of their friendship, she was in danger. Charlie may think it was his fault for leaving her alone but Sebastian knew where the blame really belonged.

Right at his feet.

He would do anything to save her, even resist Bianca.

A cool hand on his arm jolted him awake. He sat up.

"Alexa?"

"Sorry." Jessica sat down on the bed beside him. "I'm glad you got some sleep. You're going to need to be as strong as possible."

He rubbed sleep from his eyes. The last shreds of a dream drifted from his mind. He was taking an exam on a course he'd never signed up for. The students were every person he'd ever met and his mother sat at the front, keeping time. He'd entered the room to find he only had fifteen minutes left and all he had to write with was a grey crayon. Charlie and Alexa sat on either side busy at work on the exam and when he sat down, Bianca had turned around from the desk in front of him and shushed him.

Too weird.

"What time is it?" he said.

"Just before eleven," she said. "We have to start figuring out how we're going to catch Bianca."

"It's simple," he said. "I have to be the bait."

She frowned and nodded. "Yes, I think that's the only thing we can do."

"You agree with that?"

"I've tried to think of something else but we don't have time to track her properly. I'd need a few days and we don't have time. We have to get her now."

She stood up and pulled off her backpack. "As I said, I've been getting supplies." She pulled out a plastic bag and from that, pulled out a ball of silver twine, a small dart gun, and a small box that looked decidedly medical.

"What's that?" Sebastian said, picking up the box.

She plucked it out of his hands. "It's Ketamine, a powerful horse tranquilizer. A big enough dose has been known to slow vampires down. Not stop them. And by slow down, I mean for maybe a couple of minutes, if we're lucky. It might be long enough to get this on her." She held up the twine.

"Silver twine?"

"Exactly. Silver."

His eyes widened. "This is all silver?"

"Enough to hold her. That along with the drug should be enough to make her easy enough to handle. I'd prefer chains but we don't have a lot of time and without Frank, my resources are limited."

She gathered everything and put them back into the plastic bag, which she stuffed into the backpack.

"Constantine said he'll call at sunset. Talk him into meeting at the planetarium at three or four am. The later the better. He'll know that and push for earlier. Don't accept anything earlier than one."

"I want it earlier," he said.

"No, that gives him the advantage of more night time. We want the meet to be as close to dawn as we can get."

"Oh, right." He nodded. "Wait, he can't call me."

"Why? What do you mean?"

He stared at his hands in his lap, tightening into fists. "I broke my phone, remember?"

"Do you have access to another cell phone?" she said.

"Yours?"

She shook her head and stood up from the bed, backing away. "No, I can't. I'm sorry."

"Why not?"

"I can't compromise the In-Between. Not even for your friend. I'm sorry." She gestured at Charlie's empty bed. "What about your friend?"

"Yeah, that's good. Alexa has his number programmed in to hers as well."

"Okay, call and leave a voicemail with that number."

He used the dorm phone at the end of the hall. He shivered as he listened to Alexa's voice on the voicemail. She sounded so bubbly, so normal, how she'd been before this nightmare started. He left Charlie's number and returned to his room.

"When Charlie gets back, we'll borrow his cell phone," Jessica said.

"He won't just let us take it," Sebastian said. "He wants to come too."

"No." She shook her head. "He can't. That's a bad idea."

"He's coming," Sebastian said. "He won't be talked out of it."

"Do you want your friends to die?" she said. "Taking him with us is tantamount to killing him. We can't protect him and retrieve Alexa at the same time."

The door opened behind her and Charlie stepped in. He stood in the doorway, one hand on the doorknob, the other holding his textbooks. He looked from one to the other.

"Everything set?"

"Yes," Jessica said. "Can I use your phone?"

"Um, okay." Charlie fished in his pocket and pulled it out. He handed it to her.

She plucked it out of his palm and shoved it in her pocket. "Thanks."

"I thought you wanted to use it," Charlie said.

"I do. Tonight. Sebastian broke his phone so we left your number for Constantine to call." She stepped around him. "Let's go," she called back to Sebastian.

Charlie dumped his books on his bed. "I'm coming too."

Jessica turned in the doorway. "No, you're not."

"Oh yes I am," he said. "Sebastian, tell her. We've already had this discussion."

"Charlie, it might be a good idea for you to wait here…"

"No! I said I'm coming and that's it!" He glared at both of them.

Jessica shook her head. "Forget it. Don't even think of following us."

"I don't have to follow you, you're going to the old planetarium."

Her lips thinned as she turned to Sebastian. He spread his hands.

"I didn't think…"

"Obviously," she said.

"I'm coming with you and that's it," Charlie said.

"You'll just be another target," she said. "I can't look out for you."

"You won't have to."

She looked over at Sebastian. He chewed the inside of his cheek. He didn't want Charlie to come along any more than she did but what could they say to stop him? He never should have told his friend where they were planning to go. It was too good a location to change now.

"Fine." Her tone suggested it was anything but fine. "You stay back and keep out of the way. I won't be able to look after you."

"So don't," Charlie said.

She stared at him for a long moment, then turned and stomped out the door.

"Nice to see she's reasonable," Charlie said. He grabbed his jean jacket and shrugged it on.

"Charlie," Sebastian said.

"Don't." Charlie held up one finger. "Don't even say it."

Sebastian sighed. "Okay."

He knew he'd regret not trying to talk Charlie out of it, he just didn't know how much.

CHAPTER THIRTEEN

They spent the afternoon casing the old planetarium. Low hanging clouds blocked the sun for the most of the day, giving Sebastian a slight reprieve from the debilitating effects of sunshine. He still kept the sunglasses on his face and a low level headache throbbed in his temples, causing his shoulders to hunch up and his neck to ache. He lagged behind while Charlie and Jessica checked out the fencing surrounding the planetarium. At a section facing the trees, Jessica pulled out a set of wire cutters and cut a hole in the fence. They climbed through and hurried to the planetarium, crouching to make sure no one noticed.

Finding a way in took a little longer than they'd hoped but inside, the cool darkness gave Sebastian a welcome reprieve from the sun. Even with the clouds, he thought his sensitivity was getting worse. Would there come a time when he wouldn't be able to go outside during the day at all? He wouldn't be much better than a vampire. Well, except for the whole blood thing.

"Any security?" Jessica said.

"I think the campus security includes this place in their rounds at night," Charlie said. "But that's it."

"Good. You guys stay out of my way."

Jessica moved deeper in the darkness. Sebastian watched her take off her backpack and pulled small items out as she moved. The overpowering scent of garlic rose as she clenched her hand. A glass bottle glinted in her other hand before she turned away.

Charlie moved his head back and forth as if he'd lost sight of her. Of course, he had in this darkness.

"What's she doing?" Charlie whispered to him.

"I'm not sure," Sebastian said. But he had an idea.

"Shh, keep your voice down."

"Don't bother, I can hear you." Her voice floated through the air from the other side of the dome.

"Geez," said Charlie. "Where is she?"

"Over by the back wall," Sebastian said. "At the end of the platform."

Charlie turned to look at him. "You can't see that. Can you?"

"Yes, I can."

Charlie didn't say anything else after that.

By the time Jessica finished, it was late afternoon. She sent Charlie out for food. He returned forty-five minutes later with a bucket of chicken and fries. As Charlie dove in, Sebastian felt Jessica watching him as he picked at a leg and some fries. His stomach churned with every nibble but he forced himself to continue. Finally he managed to finish the leg and half the fries. He started to push his paper plate away but Jessica pulled out a breast piece and dumped it on the plate.

"Now that," she said.

"I can't," he said. "I've had enough."

"You haven't eaten a full meal's worth of food since Thursday, have you?" she said. "Don't deny it, I can tell. Your sensitivities are getting worse. Eating regular food will help arrest that, so eat it."

He felt Charlie staring at him too now. Fine, he would try. He pulled the plate back onto his lap. The chicken smelled greasy. The skin was slippery in his fingers. He lifted it and took a small bite. The texture was rubbery in his mouth and slimy on his tongue. But as with everything else, it had no flavor. He felt his stomach gurgle but he forced himself to swallow. Jessica tilted her head. He took another bite.

Every swallow made his stomach grumble more. Bile burned the back of his throat, adding a sourness to his mouth. He was almost glad of it, at least it was a flavor. He managed to eat more than half of it before he had to push the plate away.

"No more," he said.

"Okay," she said. "That was a good effort. Keep at it. It gets easier."

He didn't believe her.

Charlie was gathering the remains of their meals when a muffled ringing sounded. He dropped the paper plates and hurried over as Jessica pulled the cell phone from her pocket. She handed it to Sebastian.

"He'll want to talk to you," she said. "Remember, insist on this location and as close to dawn as possible."

Sebastian nodded and took the phone. He hit the answer button and brought it to his ear. His palm was already sweating as he held it.

"Hello?"

"Tell me, Sebastian, why am I having to call a different number to speak to you?" Constantine's voice sounded amused.

"I broke my phone," Sebastian said. "I'm using a friend's."

"Yes, Charlie. Alexa has mentioned him."

Sebastian turned away from Jessica and Charlie. He took a few steps and closed his eyes.

"Is she okay?"

"She's fine and will remain that way as long as you do what you're told."

Constantine's voice was smooth and even but Sebastian could detect a hint of an accent. English? Definitely foreign. Pronunciation too crisp and clean. It was irritating.

"I'll get Bianca," Sebastian said. "I'll bring her to the old planetarium on the edge of the campus. Alexa knows it."

Constantine laughed. "Dictating terms now?"

"It'll be easier than anywhere else. I'll have to lure Bianca here. I can't guarantee that I can hang onto her longer than it'll take to bring her here. I can't go traipsing around the city, dragging her along."

He held his breath, waiting. Would Constantine believe him? It sounded reasonable. It couldn't be that easy to contain and transport a vampire.

"Why lure Bianca there?" Constantine said.

"I'm going to where she first bit me," Sebastian said. "She's already found me there before. I'm sure she'll find me again."

Silence sounded over the phone. Even with his advanced hearing, he couldn't hear Constantine breathing. Did vampires even need to breathe? He had no idea. God, there were so many things he didn't know!

He could feel his heart start to pound and sweat trickled down his sides. Steady. He had to be calm for Alexa. It was the only way. He tipped the phone away from his mouth and took deep breaths.

"Fine." Constantine's voice startled him. "We will meet in your planetarium at midnight tonight."

"It has to be later," Sebastian said. "Three or four."

"Midnight," Constantine said. "You pick the location but I pick the time. You either be there at midnight or the next time you see Alexa, she'll have a rather toothy smile for you."

The phone clicked off in Sebastian's ear. His arm flopped down to his side.

"What'd he say?" Charlie said.

"Midnight," Jessica said. "Not even close to ideal."

Sebastian whirled on her. "I did my best. He's going to be here then whether I am or not so I'm damn well going to be."

"Easy, take it easy." Charlie stepped forward, reaching for Sebastian's shoulder. "Let's stay focused. What's the next step?" He looked over at Jessica. "So? What do we do next?"

Jessica crossed her arms over her chest. "We have to trap Bianca. And for that you're going to listen to me."

〜

So here he was again, under the trees. Hard to believe only a few short days ago he wouldn't have been able to see the detail in the trunks around him or smell the different scents of the decaying leaves and small animals that traversed the area. It seemed so long ago, a different person, a different life.

He could never go back. He knew that now. He belonged to the night, to this darkness that surrounded him. He'd never feel fully comfortable in the day again.

But he still owed it to that former life to do all he could to save Alexa. He couldn't let her be a victim of his curse.

He took another few steps. Jessica had told him to try to find the exact place where Bianca had first attacked him, or get as close as he could. He focused on the position of the trees when he'd woken up with the three guys around him. The memory was hazy.

He focused.

Remember.

He stepped out into the small clearing, really just a wider space between several trees. He felt the movement of the air on the nape of his neck, saw the way the leaves shifted on the branches above his head. The scent of decaying vegetation was still strong here under the trees but soon as spring turned to summer, the ground would dry out and absorb the dead leaves as mulch. New grass would spring up. Along the path, flowers would be planted. Maybe a few of their spores would travel into this area with the trees and take root.

But he wouldn't be here to see it. He didn't know where he'd be.

Still no sign of Bianca. He would have to follow Jessica's suggestion. He didn't want to but it didn't look like he had any other choice.

He pulled the tiny switchblade from his pocket and opened it. The blade glimmered in the dark, catching the smallest amount of light. Or maybe it was just his vision, able to see so perfectly in the dark. He rolled up the sleeve of his jacket and pressed the blade to his skin. He hated the sight of blood so he turned his face away.

The knife burned through his skin. The pain made him hiss. He felt the warm trickle on his forearm. It would be like a flashing sign to Bianca. She wouldn't be able to resist.

Sure enough, a few moments later he heard a single step from behind. He started to turn.

She hit him from the left, trapping his arm against his body. His leg buckled and they fell to the forest floor. The sickly sour of her breath filled his nostrils. He heard the snap of her teeth an inch from his neck.

His right arm was caught under his body. He wiggled, shaking his head, preventing her from biting him. Her hand grabbed his head, halting the movement. He felt the strength in her as she forced him to turn his head, exposing his neck. She bent over, her breath on his neck.

He got his hand free and slashed with the blade. He caught her on the cheek, slicing through her skin. She shrieked and reared back. He pulled the handcuffs from his left pocket and snapped one onto her right arm. Then he yanked her left hand down and snapped the other cuff on her left wrist.

She pulled back, teetered on her feet and then fell back on her rump. She held her hands out in front of her and started to laugh.

"You really think these will hold me?" she said. "I can snap these in half as quickly as I can snap your neck."

"Not quite that fast."

He pulled out a spool and wrapped the silver wire around her wrists and the cuffs. She screamed. He noticed tiny puffs of smoke rising from her wrists.

Jessica jumped out from behind the trees opposite him. She ran forward and stuffed a gag in Bianca's mouth, shutting off the screams. She used her own spool of silver wire to secure the gag. Then she and Sebastian wrapped more of the silver wire around her body, locking her arms against her torso. Behind the gag, Bianca screamed. She shook her head from side to side, trying to dislodge the gag but only causing the wire to rub against her cheeks and head. More smoke trickled up from any part of her skin exposed to the wire.

Jessica pulled a needle from her pocket and jammed it into Bianca`s leg. Her thumb stabbed at the plunger. Bianca howled into her gag.

"Stop struggling," Jessica said. "It'll hurt less."

Finally Bianca stopped. She sagged on the ground, her chest heaving. Vampires do breathe, Sebastian realized, watching her. He tied another strand of silver wire to the handcuffs and trailed it off like a lead. Then he and Jessica stood on either side and helped Bianca to her feet.

Behind them, a flashlight appeared, shining on the ground as Charlie entered the area. He shone the beam forward, leading the way.

"Let's go," Jessica said.

They stayed on either side, each holding onto one of Bianca's arms as they followed Charlie. Sebastian could see his friend looking back every once in a while at Bianca, his eyes showing white in the darkness. Sebastian smelled the fear dripping off Charlie. Bianca's muscles tensed under his hands; she smelled it too. She made a growling sound in her throat. Sebastian jerked on the wires, making them rub her skin. Her flesh hissed, turning her growl into a whine.

"Don't even think about it," he said. She looked at him and he saw the rage burning in her eyes.

He kind of felt the same about her.

They reached the chain link fence. Charlie stepped back, shining the beam at the section Jessica had cut through earlier that day. Jessica slid through first and held the fencing back. Both she and Sebastian manoeuvred Bianca through, twisting and turning her to make sure she didn't get caught on the wire. She grunted and growled low through her gag.

Once through, Sebastian checked her bindings then nodded to Jessica.

"I'll take her from here."

"There's still time," Jessica said. "I can help you take her in and then leave."

"It's okay," he said. "I don't want to take the chance that they see you."

She pressed her lips together. In the darkness, her hair was a dark curtain around her pale face.

"You know it's a trap," she said. "You know..."

He held up a hand to stop her. He didn't want to hear what he knew she'd say. He couldn't bring himself to think it and he didn't want to hear it spoken aloud.

"I have to," he said. "I just have to try."

She nodded. "Good luck then."

"Thanks."

He took Bianca's arm and steered her toward the looming shape of the planetarium.

Inside the stench of rotting carpeting, dust and mould filled his nostrils, drowning out the smell of Charlie's fear and the lingering scent of Jessica's shampoo. Bianca slipped on the uneven floor and he had to support her. Even through the rag, he could smell the sourness of her breath. He could feel the power in her muscles under his hands as he guided her to the front of the planetarium. The drug was beginning to wear off. Now she was biding her time, he knew. At the right moment, she would try to make a break for it. Just as long as he could hold onto her until Constantine came, then in the resulting chaos Sebastian would get Alexa away.

He had it all cunningly planned out, as if it might happen that way. Right.

They reached the front of the planetarium, near a small podium that sagged and listed to the right. The dark was even thicker inside and yet he could still see, better than he ever had in daylight. The sourness of Bianca's breath drew thicker and he realized she'd chewed through her gag.

"The night feels better, doesn't it?" Her voice purred in his ear.

He tightened his grip on her arm, now holding her away from him.

"It's Constantine who asked you to bring me here," she said. "This sounds like one of his plans. Is there a hostage? He'll betray that, you know. That's how he does things."

"Shut up," Sebastian said.

She laughed, her voice tinkling out into the darkness and echoing back in weird distortion.

"Do you really think you can outsmart him? Finish turning with me and we can go against him together."

"You shouldn't talk about outsmarting him," Sebastian said. "Your plans didn't exactly work."

"I just didn't have enough time with you," she said. "If I hadn't been interrupted, you wouldn't have suffered. I can fix that now."

"Shut up," he said.

"With the two of us..."

"He told you to shut up, Bianca." A deep voice sounded from behind them. "You still have trouble obeying that."

Sebastian spun around, dragging Bianca with him. She stumbled but righted herself.

Behind them, Constantine stood with two other men behind him. The two flanked Alexa on either side, holding her arms. She looked dishevelled, hair messed, tears and dirt streaked her cheeks. Her clothing looked soiled and torn.

Sebastian's heart pounded at the sight of her. His fault, all of it his fault. If she was injured...

Stop, focus, he had to stay calm.

A cold smile curled Constantine's lips. He took a step forward, spreading his hands in a supplicating gesture.

"I'm so pleased you are on time and brought Bianca," he said. "I believe we will be able to conclude our arrangement satisfactorily."

"We're here," Sebastian said. "Let Alexa go. That was the arrangement."

Constantine held up one hand. "Not so fast. I've gotten quite fond of her." He moved his hand back toward her. The two men on either side of Alexa propelled her forward until she was close enough for Constantine to stroke her face. She didn't even move, Sebastian noticed. She must be terrified.

"Idiot," Bianca whispered. "Do you really think he'll let her go? He never lets anyone go."

Constantine's smile widened. "What tall tales are you telling now, Bianca?"

She glared at him and he laughed.

"I'll give you Bianca," Sebastian said. "You let Alexa go."

"Hmm, interesting. Let me consider it a moment." Constantine made a show of stroking his bearded chin, tilting his head to the ceiling.

"I may have gone along with your idea if you hadn't disobeyed my instructions," he said.

"What are you talking about?" Sebastian said. "I'm here, I brought Bianca."

"And you were to come alone," Constantine said. "Not with friends."

A shout sounded behind Sebastian. Then came the sound of furniture crashing over. He turned his head and saw a large man grab Charlie from a pile of broken chairs and hurl him farther toward the podium. Charlie almost flew through the air, his feet trying to reach the ground before he landed among another group of chairs. Dust and dirt filled the air, mixed with the unmistakable scent of blood. The large man grabbed Charlie and held him up like a rag doll.

"That's enough," Constantine said. "Did you get the other one?"

From Constantine's right, two more vampires emerged, dragging

Jessica. She struggled against them but they held her fast. At Constantine's signal, the two vampires stopped. Even from this distance, Sebastian could see the muscle jumping in her jaw as she clenched her teeth.

"Idiot," Bianca said.

"He's just a college student," Constantine said. "He couldn't be expected to know any better. And you, my dear, do you really think I'm going to let another abomination like you survive?" He spoke this directly to Jessica.

"He's more like you than me," Jessica said. "You might want to be careful around him."

Constantine scowled at her.

Too far, Sebastian thought, it had all gone too far and it had even started out that way. He had to figure out a way to get Alexa and Charlie out of here. He wanted Jessica out of here too but he didn't think that would be possible. At least she might have a chance to survive this encounter. Neither Alexa or Charlie could say the same.

"Let Alexa and Charlie go," Sebastian said. "You do that and I won't resist you."

Constantine's attention shifted to him and he again felt the pressure of the vampire's power pressing down on him. It made him want to cower, to hide, to admit he didn't know anything, he was just a regular college student who couldn't even stop spilling food all over himself. But Alexa stood just off to the side, surrounded by vampires and Charlie sagged to his left, barely able to stand and bleeding from several small wounds.

Sebastian couldn't crumple with them around. They needed him, needed him to be strong, to be stronger than he'd ever been before.

He felt Constantine's power almost like physical blows, pounding against him, trying to batter him down. He saw Jessica turn her head, cringing. Charlie covered his head with his arms. Beside him, Bianca whimpered, shaking her head, trying to inch back, away from that black presence, pushing down and down, demanding obedience, demanding sacrifice, demanding oblivion.

And Sebastian stood against it.

He felt his stomach curl inside himself. His body hunched but he kept his gaze locked on Constantine. His hand gripping Bianca's arm tightened, pinching her skin. She whined and tried to pull away but his grip was steel. His other hand clenched into a fist so tight that his nails broke through the skin on his palm. Blood dripped to the ruined carpet. He could feel the vampires' interest shift, even Constantine's. Just one more moment. Beside him, Bianca leaned forward and craned her neck to look around him.

He grabbed her with both arms and shoved her up and forward. The throw carried her over halfway toward Constantine and momentum carried her the rest of the way. Constantine stepped back, catching her in his arms. Sebastian sprinted to the wall by the podium. He punched the switch.

The mixture of holy water and garlic sprayed from the few remaining water sprinklers. Only half of the podium area got hit but the water splashed up. It struck the legs of the vampire holding Charlie. It shrieked and dropped him as it tried to flee. One of the sprays hit Jessica and the vampires holding her square on. They screamed and started smoking even before they dropped Jessica's arms and staggered back.

Sebastian ran toward Alexa as the vampires around her howled in agony. She was crying herself as he reached her. His arm wrapped around her shoulder and he pulled her away. Bianca shrieked then he heard the sound of crashing glass and wood. He listened for Constantine's bellow but never heard it. He aimed straight for the door.

Sebastian burst through, dragging Alexa with him. He led her across the uneven drive toward the hole in the fence. Once through, he grabbed her hand and they ran. He didn't look back. He had to trust that Jessica got Charlie out. She'd promised him she would.

His feet devoured the ground beneath them. Occasionally Alexa stumbled and he had to slow to let her catch up, then he ran full out again, dragging her along. Finally they reached the cover of the trees and he stopped.

She sagged against a nearby tree. Her legs folded beneath her and she sat on the ground, her head bowed. Sebastian stood over her, gulping in air, trying to get his heart to stop pounding so hard. But she was here. They'd done it. Somehow it had worked.

Alexa was safe.

"It's okay, Alexa," he said. "You're okay now."

She nodded. "Yes."

He knelt down to look her in the face. She bowed her head, her eyes lost in the shadows. He wanted to touch her just once. His hand lifted to stroke her cheek then lowered. He didn't have the right to start anything he couldn't finish. But he couldn't just leave without saying anything.

"Alexa," he said. Her head tilted. He could tell she was listening.

He heard footsteps a moment later. He reached for the knife in his pocket but then caught a whiff of Charlie's sweat. Jessica appeared from behind some bushes. Charlie's arm was draped across her shoulders. He gave Sebastian a wavering thumbs up.

"Charlie," Alexa said.

"Hey Alexa." Charlie staggered a step and then flopped on the ground beside her. "You got to keep hanging out with us. That was a lousy class of folks you were just with."

Jessica moved forward, her hands resting on her hips.

"That was a good plan," Sebastian said.

Jessica smiled. "I thought it might work, especially when I saw the piping."

"It was a really good idea," Alexa said. "Mostly."

"Mostly?" Charlie said. "What are you talking about? It was perfect. Except that I feel like I could sleep for a week."

"You'll have longer than that." Alexa turned her face toward Charlie. He wrinkled his nose as if he smelled something sour.

Something like breath...

Sebastian sucked in air to yell but Alexa was already moving. She fell on Charlie, driving him down to the ground. She lunged at his neck. He screamed. The scream ended in a gurgle as she ripped his throat open. Blood sprayed up, soaking the side of her face as she drank.

"No!" Sebastian grabbed her shoulders and yanked. Alexa came up still holding Charlie in a lethal embrace, her face buried in his neck. Jessica slapped her face, breaking her grip. Charlie fell back to the ground. Sebastian dragged Alexa away. Her elbow shot back, digging into his stomach. His grip loosened as the pain exploded in him. She broke away, darted toward the tree. She spun to face them. Blood smeared across her chin and cheeks. Her mouth opened in a sneer, revealing her fangs.

"You didn't really think it would be so simple, did you?"

Constantine's voice filtered through the darkness. A shadow appeared through the trees as he stepped out into the clearing. "You didn't really think I would just give her back? She is so sweet and delectable. I just had to keep her."

His laughter echoed through the clearing. Sebastian watched a familiar smile spread across Alexa's face. Constantine held a hand out to her and she moved toward him, her movements smooth and gliding, a supernatural parody of her human self.

"Poor Sebastian," she said. "You waited too long. I would have said yes, you know. But not now." Her nose wrinkled as if she smelled something distasteful. "Now you wouldn't taste very good." She lifted her hand and licked blood from her fingers. "Charlie tasted quite yummy."

Her laughter pierced him. He felt hands holding him back as he tried to lunge forward.

Constantine took Alexa's arm. "You really should have let yourself finish, boy," he said. "You were a good choice although I'll have to chastise Bianca for her impudence. Your little stunt with the water let her get away. I have to go deal with her. My reputation, you see. But don't worry. I won't forget about you, boy. Not at all."

He caressed Alexa's cheek with his thin fingers. She smiled, revealing her fangs, pressing her body to his side.

"But I do thank you for my new addition. She's quite delectable."

He laughed, curling his fingers in her hand. They melted away into the shadows. Alexa's answering laughter faded in the breeze, leaving behind a deathly silence.

"Stop Sebastian, you can't go after them. Not now." Jessica's voice spoke over and over in his ear. She tugged at his arms, trying to turn him away. Finally his gaze fell on Charlie. He broke away from Jessica and dropped to his knees by his friend. Maybe there was still time, maybe if they got him to the emergency room, a blood transfusion, suture up his neck...

Charlie's skin already felt cold. His eyes stared unseeing up at the canopy of leaves above their heads. Blood coated his torn neck and soaked his t-shirt and jeans jacket. It no longer pulsed out as his heart had stopped pumping.

A hand tightened on Sebastian's shoulder.

"Come on," Jessica said. "We have to go."

She took his arm and led him away.

CHAPTER FOURTEEN

The day of Charlie's funeral dawned overcast and grey. Sebastian insisted on attending, even though the sunlight still made him feel weak and nauseous. He stood well back from the crowd, dark sunglasses on his face. He wore a dark suit, if only for the opportunity to keep as much of himself covered as possible.

Jessica stood beside him, her brown hair loose from her usual ponytail. It flowed across her shoulders like a curtain. She didn't seem quite so bothered by the sunlight, although she did wear long sleeves and solid colored stockings under her skirt.

Sebastian had never met Charlie's parents. He spotted them easily, huddled together at the graveside. Charlie's father had the same dirty blond hair, just shorter and more tamed. His lined face hinted at the man Charlie might have become. But no longer.

The official story was animal attack. No person could have made those wounds. Sebastian didn't hear the rumors floating around the school; he didn't have access anymore. He hadn't returned to the dorm and skipped his classes.

Jessica had them booked on a flight tomorrow. Somewhere in Europe, he hadn't paid attention to where, just as long as it was out of here and as far away as possible.

If only he could leave himself behind.

The minister's voice, a droning murmur, finally ceased. The sobs of Charlie's mother filled the silence. A breeze rustled the grass and the trees in the distance. It brought the scent of fresh earth to Sebastian's nostrils. He caught a whiff of Charlie's mother's perfume.

The shadows lightened as the sun poked out from behind a cloud, showering the area with golden light. Sebastian felt pain stab through his temples and tighten his scalp.

Jessica touched his arm. "We should go."

He shook his head. He didn't want to leave, even with the pain starting to twist his stomach. He deserved it, deserved all of it. He should have forced Charlie to stay behind. He should never have left Alexa alone. He'd been stupid and thoughtless.

He wished Bianca had finished the job that night just over a week ago. At least then Charlie and Alexa would still be alive, even if he wasn't.

Jessica tugged on his arm again and this time he turned to follow her. His feet moved along without him thinking about it. If only he could stop thinking for good, just move and breathe, let Jessica position him like a doll. But the thoughts kept coming, the memories popped into his head at odd moments. Waking up in the morning to see Charlie sprawled diagonally across his bed, his head where his feet should be, mouth open as he snored. Alexa sitting beside him in class, twirling a pencil, her tongue poking out the tiniest bit between her lips as she contemplated a difficult question, her glasses slipping halfway down her nose as she peered over the frames. Sitting in the bar, the three of them laughing, drinking cheap beer and eating greasy nachos. He still remembered the spicy flavor of the salsa and the way Alexa would lick her fingers.

And he always ended up with spots of salsa staining his shirt.

He felt tears on his cheeks. The sunlight must be making his eyes water. Yes, that had to be it.

"Are you sure an email wouldn't be better?" Jessica said. "Maybe a phone call?"

"I can't talk to them," Sebastian said. "There'd be too many questions about things I can't answer."

She shrugged and turned away, continuing to pack her small suitcase. He checked the letter one last time, reviewing what he'd written to his parents. He'd already laid the ground work with his original email to them the day after Charlie's death. They wouldn't be happy about Sebastian dropping out of school so close to the end of the year. He could almost see his father's sour expression. He would grumble about cost and the future and mistakes. His mother would try to get his father to see that Sebastian wouldn't be able to concentrate on his studies anyway. His brother was too young and interested in video games to notice. Sebastian had already made cursory visits to the registrar, placing his year on hold. He would be able to return and finish the year when he was able. He'd made sure to put that in the letter to his parents.

He didn't mention that he would never go back.

A regular life wasn't possible anymore.

How could he be regular when he was half-vampire, when he knew the things he knew, had seen the things he'd seen? How could he pretend everything was all right when his best friend was dead and the woman he loved had been turned into a monster?

Alexa had been reported as missing when she didn't return to her dorm after a few days. Police were already investigating and had left messages for him at his dorm. Sebastian had no intention of talking to them. What could he say?

He reviewed his letter to his parents one last time. He imagined his mother reading it and then passing it along to his father. Her hand would go up to her throat, playing with the silver chain she always wore around her neck. It was a wonder she hadn't broken it with the twisting. He could almost hear his little brother, Callum, asking what was in the letter and his parents telling him not to worry about it. That would only make Callum wonder more and then start to worry. If it was possible, Callum was even more serious and awkward than Sebastian, but he was super bright. At thirteen, he could easily be in his last year of high school but insisted on staying in the same grade as his friends.

He just decided to take every class in his grade.

Sebastian closed his eyes. He had to let them go. He had to let them all go. They were part of an old life.

He took a breath and opened his eyes. He folded the letter and inserted it in an envelope. He checked the postage again and sealed it.

"What time is the flight?" he said.

"Six fifteen," Jessica said. "We should be at the airport around three."

"Okay," he said. "I have some place to go first."

~≈~

She wanted to go with him but he wouldn't let her. He knew she didn't believe his excuse of wanting to mail the letter but she relented after making sure he carried her cell phone. He knew it was a false precaution. If anything was going to happen, no call would bring help fast enough.

He dropped the letter in a post box three blocks from the cemetery. Black iron fencing bordered the cemetery, rising several feet above his head, the tips hardened into pointed spears. He had to wait for a few cars to drive by before there was enough of a break for him to scale the fence. As he dropped down, landing in a crouch, another car drove by, its headlights sweeping across the front of the cemetery before moving on down the road. He waited a moment to see if the car came back but the road stayed quiet. Midnight wasn't a popular time to drive past a cemetery.

Standing up, he turned his back on the road and headed deeper inside. Finding Charlie's grave was easy. His night vision was now perfect. He picked out details and features that had missed him even when he'd been fully human. That headstone there had the tiniest flaws along the left side, creating a surface just a smidge rougher than the right side. The grass toward the back of the cemetery was just a centimeter or so longer than the grass at the front.

The caretaker didn't take as much care near the back.

The scent of fresh earth and the hint of decay drew him to Charlie's grave. The mound of earth looked raw and exposed compared to the manicured green surrounding it. Charlie's parents had spent the money to buy Charlie a full sized upright headstone. The rush job to get it engraved must have cost a small fortune as well.

A breeze rustled the grass and stirred a few specks of dirt on the top of the mound. Sebastian pushed his hair back from his eyes. Over the scent of earth and decay, he smelled a familiar sour stench.

He hadn't heard her approach but he probably shouldn't have expected to. He turned to see Alexa standing a distance away beneath a tree. She still wore the same shirt, pastel pink, now stained dark with Charlie's blood.

"I didn't mean it to be him," she said. Her voice carried even this distance. She sounded like she was standing right next to him.

"You meant it to be someone else?" he said.

"You know what I mean," she said. "I needed to feed. It's overwhelming at first. You can't control it. I'm sorry it was Charlie."

He shook his head. "Stop pretending that you're her. You aren't."

She moved now, circling around toward the back of the cemetery, never getting closer but never getting away.

"I am Alexa," she said. "It isn't that big a change. Not really. It's just a little farther for you. You should think about it, Sebastian. If you turned, we could be together. You want that, don't you?"

He stared at her.

"I want it too. I never told you that. I wanted you to say it. I kept waiting for you to and I think you were just about to, weren't you? I always wondered why you didn't."

He couldn't take his eyes off her. The wind tousled her hair the way it always did, messing up the part. She even tugged at her sleeves the same way. She used to complain that her arms were too long or the sleeves were too short, so she tugged on them, even when they were long enough. And even now as a vampire, she tugged on her sleeves.

As if she was still Alexa.

As if she was still the woman he loved.

But she wasn't.

The woman he loved couldn't have murdered his best friend and then apologized so casually. She couldn't have talked about any of this while he stood less than a foot from that friend's new grave.

"I was afraid to," he said. "But I'm not anymore. Maybe you're right. Maybe I should finish it."

She smiled, a familiar twisting of the mouth but nothing shifted in her eyes. She began to move forward, closing the distance between them. As she drew closer, he saw a paleness under the olive tone of her skin. Her hair hung just a little limper on her head.

"You're so close," she said. "I can smell it in you. I can't drink you because *she* was the one who started it but if you drink from me, that will complete the turning. Then we can be together."

"Yes," he said.

He held his arms loose at his side. The sleeves of his leather jacket hung to his wrists. His feet were just about shoulder width apart.

She kept smiling as she moved closer. She began rolling up the sleeve of her pink top, exposing the pale olive flesh of forearm. He caught a whiff of the fading scent of her floral perfume.

It did nothing to hide the sour smell.

From ten feet away, he could the tips of her fangs against her pale lips as she smiled. From five feet away, the sourness of her was almost overwhelming. She held out her arm, raising it up to the level of his mouth.

"Taste," she said.

He moved. Slashing with the silver knife that dropped into his hand from his sleeve. But she was too far away. She jumped back. He missed her chest but the blade sliced through her arm. She shrieked as the silver blade cut deep. Smoke sizzled from the cut in her arm. She grabbed her arm with her other hand. She snarled at him as she crouched, protecting herself. Her fangs glinted in the moonlight.

"You're not Alexa," he said. "She's gone. But I'll kill you for what you did to Charlie and for wearing her face."

He lunged again but the vampire darted away. This time she turned and ran, holding her wounded arm. The echo of her footsteps thumping away on the ground faded in the distance.

He tried to follow but she was too fast. He stopped chasing after a few minutes, then stumbled back to Charlie's grave. He stood with his hands on his knees gasping for breath. His heart pounded so loud in his ears he didn't hear anything until she spoke.

"Nice try but you should have waited until she got closer, maybe even put your mouth up to her arm. As long you didn't bite down and swallow any blood you would've been okay."

He looked up. Jessica tilted her head. Her pony tail flopped over her shoulder.

"You followed me," he said.

"Of course I did. Didn't think I was going to let you come out here alone, did you?"

"I just had to... I mean... I needed to..."

She nodded. "I know. You had to see if there was any part of her left."

He straightened. The pounding of his heart had turned into a dull ache. "Yeah, but there wasn't."

"There never is," she said. "Can I have my knife back now?"

She held out her hand. He stepped forward and handed it over, handle out. She took it and slipped it into the sheath at her waist. Then she slipped her arm through his, turning him away from Charlie's grave.

"If you're going to use a knife, you're going to need to learn to use it better," she said. "You just don't go waving it around."

"Could you teach me?" he said.

"Some. And what I don't know, you can learn from some of the others."

He nodded. "Good. I want to learn all you know."

She stopped walking. He moved ahead and felt her hand slip from his arm. He stopped and turned to her.

"Revenge isn't a good way to live your life, Sebastian," she said.

"Maybe, but it's the only way I've got to live right now."

She sighed. "I know the feeling. Believe me. But you need to put it away for now. You've got a lot of adjusting to do."

He nodded. "Okay. Let's get our stuff and head for the airport."

She smiled, and even in the moonlight, he didn't see any hint of fangs. She stepped up and took his arm, leading him back into the darkness to a new life.

About the Author

Based in Toronto, Canada, Rebecca M. Senese writes horror, science fiction and mystery/crime, often all at once in the same story. Garnering an Honorable Mention in "The Year's Best Science Fiction" and nominated for numerous Aurora Awards, her work has appeared in *Tesseracts 16: Parnassus Unbound, Imaginarium 2012, Tesseracts 15: A Case of Quite Curious Tales, Ride the Moon, TransVersions, Deadbolt Magazine, On Spec, The Vampire's Crypt, Storyteller, Reflection's Edge, Future Syndicate* and *Into the Darkness*, amongst others.

When not serving up tales of the macabre, mysterious or wondrous, she volunteers as a zombie or vampire at haunted attractions in October to stalk and scare all the unsuspecting innocents.

Find Me Online

Website - http://www.RebeccaSenese.com
Twitter - http://twitter.com/RebeccaSenese